Silent Bite
A Scanguards Wedding

A Scanguards Vampire Novella

By Tina Folsom

1001 Dark Nights

EVIL EYE
CONCEPTS

Silent Bite: A Scanguards Wedding
A Scanguards Vampires Novella
1001 Dark Nights
By Tina Folsom

Published by Evil Eye Concepts, Incorporated

Sign up for the 1001 Dark Nights Newsletter
and be entered to win a Tiffany Key necklace.

There's a contest every month!

Visit www.1001DarkNights.com/key to subscribe.

As a bonus, all subscribers will receive a free
1001 Dark Nights story on 1/1/15.
The First Night
by Shayla Black, Lexi Blake & M.J. Rose

One Thousand and One Dark Nights

Once upon a time, in the future...

*I was a student fascinated with stories and learning.
I studied philosophy, poetry, history, the occult, and
the art and science of love and magic. I had a vast
library at my father's home and collected thousands
of volumes of fantastic tales.*

*I learned all about ancient races and bygone
times. About myths and legends and dreams of all
people through the millennium. And the more I read
the stronger my imagination grew until I discovered
that I was able to travel into the stories... to actually
become part of them.*

*I wish I could say that I listened to my teacher
and respected my gift, as I ought to have. If I had, I
would not be telling you this tale now.
But I was foolhardy and confused, showing off
with bravery.*

*One afternoon, curious about the myth of the
Arabian Nights, I traveled back to ancient Persia to
see for myself if it was true that every day Shahryar
(Persian: شهريار, "king") married a new virgin, and then
sent yesterday's wife to be beheaded. It was written
and I had read, that by the time he met Scheherazade,
the vizier's daughter, he'd killed one thousand
women.*

*Something went wrong with my efforts. I arrived
in the midst of the story and somehow exchanged
places with Scheherazade – a phenomena that had*

*never occurred before and that still to this day, I
cannot explain.*

*Now I am trapped in that ancient past. I have
taken on Scheherazade's life and the only way I can
protect myself and stay alive is to do what she did to
protect herself and stay alive.*

*Every night the King calls for me and listens as I spin tales.
And when the evening ends and dawn breaks, I stop at a
point that leaves him breathless and yearning for more.
And so the King spares my life for one more day, so that
he might hear the rest of my dark tale.*

*As soon as I finish a story... I begin a new
one... like the one that you, dear reader, have before
you now.*

1

At the sight of Ursula's pale neck, Oliver felt a shiver race down his spine and shoot into his balls like a lance. It was a pleasurable kind of pain that he experienced: intense, yet at the same time he didn't want it to stop.

His fingers elongated, and his fingernails turned into sharp barbs. They were the claws of a beast because that's what he still was inside, what he would always be, despite his refined exterior and the gentle shell he wore for everybody.

Ursula was the only one who knew better because she saw it every day and every night: the hunger that still simmered so closely under the surface. The insatiable hunger for blood. But it was different now.

Right after his turning, he'd sunk his fangs into any neck that was unfortunate enough to cross his path. Now, over half a year later, his taste had become much more sophisticated. Still, there was nothing refined about it. Nothing gentle or sweet. Nor civilized.

Only one thing had changed. He cared about the woman who offered her neck night after night more than he'd ever cared about anybody. He'd fallen in love with her before ever tasting her blood, before he even truly knew her, and he wouldn't hesitate to sacrifice his own life in order to save hers.

They hadn't been apart since the night he'd first bitten her, when she'd freely offered him her vein, despite the ordeal she'd been through for three long years. Despite the disgust she'd associated with the act until then. But Ursula had pushed her fears aside and given herself to him, trusted him and put the nightmare she'd experienced at the blood brothel aside.

For him.

Because she trusted him not to hurt her.

"What's wrong?" Ursula's voice came from the closet from which she removed her clothes and packed them into several large boxes.

"This!" He pointed to the moving boxes.

She tilted her head to the side and sighed heavily, her almond-shaped eyes begging for understanding. When she pushed a strand of her straight, raven-black hair behind her shoulder, the gesture reminded him of what it felt like when he buried his face in her hair and smelled her unique scent, a scent that came from her special blood. Blood that had the power to drug a vampire. Blood so addictive that his friends and colleagues at Scanguards had tried to keep him from her when they'd first found out.

"But we agreed," she said softly.

Oliver took a step toward her, the beast inside him howling and demanding to be let out of its cage. "I know we agreed, but that doesn't mean I have to like it."

"It's not easy for me either," she replied, dropping a stack of T-shirts into a box and moving toward him with cat-like grace.

He'd always found her beautiful, ever since the first night she'd literally fallen into his arms in one of the dingiest parts of San Francisco. He realized that he'd never had a chance at resisting her, not even if her blood had been ordinary. Not even then would he have been able to disentangle himself from the Asian beauty who made his heart race whenever he looked at her.

Though his heart wasn't the only organ that coveted her.

How he was supposed to survive without her, he couldn't fathom.

"Please," she whispered when she reached him, placing her palm on his cheek. "Don't make this any harder than it is."

At her choice of words, he took her hand and slipped it to the front of his jeans, pressing it against the bulge that had formed there. The bulge that was ever present when he was near her.

"Harder?" he echoed. "I don't think it can get any harder."

Ursula chuckled. "Is that all you think of?"

Oliver slid his hand on her nape, pulling her to him. "No. I also think of not being able to do this."

He brought his lips to hers, gently pressing against her mouth. When he licked against the seam of her lips, she parted them lightly, and her breath rushed toward him.

"Hmm," she hummed.

"Won't you reconsider?" he coaxed her.

"I can't."

But he didn't want to accept her answer. "Imagine what you'll be missing." He captured her mouth fully and slid his tongue between her parted lips, exploring her warmth, dancing with her tongue.

Ursula severed her lips from his. "Oliver, we don't have time."

"Just one last time," he insisted and busied himself with tugging on her T-shirt, sliding it up her torso.

"But—"

He silenced her protest with a kiss and slid his hands underneath her shirt, caressing her soft skin. When his hands moved high up and encountered her bra, he stopped for a brief moment. Why she bothered to wear one, he wasn't sure. Her young breasts were perfectly firm and round and needed no support. Besides, she never wore it for long, because he always found a way of stripping her of it so he could caress her boobs whenever he wanted to—which was frequently.

It took Oliver all of two seconds to find the clasp of her bra and open it. Immediately, he slid his hands under her bra and cupped her breasts, squeezing them lightly.

She moaned into his mouth, and at the same time he heard her heartbeat accelerate. Touching her breasts and fondling her nipples never failed to arouse her. Even though they didn't have the time for this now, she responded to him as if her body couldn't help itself.

"There you go, baby," he murmured, releasing her lips for a brief moment. "You want this too." He inhaled her heady scent. "You can't wait to feel me inside you."

"Oliver, this is crazy. We have to get to the airport." Despite her protest, she didn't push him away but pressed her pelvis against his rigid cock.

"We have a few minutes."

And he was going to take advantage of the time they had left. Without allowing her any further protest, he pulled her T-shirt over her head and slipped the bra off her shoulders, dropping it carelessly to the floor.

"Undress me," he ordered while he gazed at her beautiful breasts that were topped with dark nipples. Hard nipples. Yes, there was no denying that she was as aroused as he.

Ursula let out a sigh.

"You know I'll make it worth your while. I always do," he whispered, pressing a kiss to her neck and grazing her skin with the sharp fangs that had already descended.

She shivered under the contact. "Oh God."

No more protests came over her lips. Instead, her hands went to work, freeing him of his shirt, then opening the button and zipper of his pants. When she pushed them over his hips, he helped her and stepped out of them. Before she could free him of his boxer briefs, he helped her take off her own pants.

She wore only a tiny G-string that barely covered any of her enticing flesh. On top of it, the material was practically see-through and hid nothing from his vampire vision.

Oliver licked his lips in anticipation of what would happen now.

He loved satisfying two of his greatest cravings at once. Two birds with one stone. Not only was it utterly thrilling to take her blood while he was inside her, in his and Ursula's case it was also necessary. Only after she achieved an orgasm would the drugging effect of her blood be muted for a short while so that imbibing on it wouldn't turn him into a crazed addict. Less than an hour after her orgasm, her blood would be just as dangerous as before and therefore off-limits to him.

Oliver slipped his hand into her panties, combing through the neatly trimmed triangle of curls that guarded her sex, and headed farther south. Warmth and wetness greeted his foraging fingers. Instantly, his cock began to jerk, wanting to feel what his fingers felt.

"Take my cock out," he ground out, impatient for her touch because no matter how often he'd made love to her in the last few months, every time was different and new. And more thrilling than the last time.

Moments later, he felt her hands push down his boxer briefs, sliding them down his legs. Then one hand wrapped around him.

"Like that?" Ursula asked with a provocative tone in her voice.

"Yes, just like that, as if you didn't know it."

She squeezed his cock in her hand, making his heart pound into his throat.

"Fuck, baby!"

He groaned loudly and threw his head back, for a moment reveling in her tender touch. Then his fingers moved, bathing themselves in her wetness before sliding higher again to where her center of pleasure resided. When he slid one finger over it, pressing lightly, her eyelids fluttered and her throat released an audible gasp. He knew her body so well, knew exactly how to make her purr like a kitten, how to make her writhe underneath him in ecstasy, and how to make her shudder in his arms. And he couldn't get enough of it, of seeing her lips curl into a sensual smile, her eyes darken with passion, and her body tremble with desire.

Because in turn it caused a reaction in him: his entire body began to burn with need, the need to possess her, to make her his forever. Desire scorched him from the inside. The smoldering embers of his love for her ignited anew every time he looked at her sinful body, every time he kissed her sensual lips and touched her silken skin. It was as if she'd bewitched him by looking at him with her almond-shaped eyes as if he were the only man who mattered to her.

Just as she looked at him now.

"Take me," she murmured, her lips barely moving. "I need to feel you."

"I thought you'd never ask."

Within seconds he'd placed her on the bed, stripped her of her panties, and spread her legs. He'd taken her every way possible in the last few months, but what he still liked best was Ursula underneath him and looking into her eyes when he drove into her. He loved seeing her reaction when he plunged into her tight pussy and stretched her. Loved the way her breath rushed out of her lungs when he drove deeper than she thought he could. Loved the way her breasts bounced from side to side and up and down with each thrust.

"Don't make me wait," Ursula begged now.

A smile built on Oliver's lips. He hadn't even noticed that he'd been simply staring at her, feasting his eyes on her beauty. "No, my love, I'll never make you wait."

Then he brought his cock to her nether lips and plunged forward, seating himself balls-deep. A shudder ran down his spine and shot into his balls, threatening to unman him. It was always like that with her. The first thrust into her tight, silken sheath always did that to him because it was the moment he remembered what he missed most when she wasn't lying in his arms, panting. He missed the way she imprisoned him within her. The way she chained him to her body and her soul with only the tiniest squeeze of her interior muscles that she was probably not even aware of.

Whenever he felt her squeeze him like that, it felt as if his heart were being squeezed in the same way. As if she held his heart in her hand. Because she did. Because his heart belonged to her.

When he felt Ursula's hands on his hips, urging him to move, he complied with her wishes, falling into a rhythm that she dictated. Slowly, he drove in and out of her, shifting his angle so that with each descent his pelvis rocked against her clit. At the beginning of their relationship, she'd had problems letting herself go, but they'd overcome that obstacle and Ursula now responded to him freely and without inhibitions, her body pushing against him to increase the pressure on her clit. He reacted to her sign and started moving faster while he tried to stave off his own need to climax, a task which became more and more difficult by the second.

He tried to distract himself, but as he looked down at her, he saw how small rivulets of sweat ran from her neck through the valley of her breasts. It made her skin glow even more intensely and her scent more powerful, drawing him to her even more.

"Oh, God, baby!" he ground out, all too aware that his fangs were at full length and itching for a bite. "I need you to come!" Only then could he plunge his fangs into her lovely neck and find his own release.

"So close," she whispered between pants.

"What do you need, baby? Tell me!"

"Please."

Her back arched off the bed, her breasts thrusting toward him. Oliver dipped his head and captured one nipple, sucked on it greedily, his fangs grazing the sensitive peak. Underneath him, Ursula shivered, her body trembling now.

He moved to the other breast, repeating the same action, while he continued driving his cock deeper into her tight pussy. His hips worked at a rapid tempo, thrusting and withdrawing in quick succession. Another few thrusts and he would be unable to hold back his need to plunge his fangs into her flesh; another few thrusts and he would take her blood and allow it to drug him despite the disaster this would spell for both of them. Despite the fact it would destroy him.

His entire body began to tremble, and he knew he'd lost. This was his doom. Ursula was his doom, just like they'd all predicted. He wasn't strong enough to resist the temptation her blood represented.

His lips widened as he set his fangs to either side of her nipple and took a last breath. He pierced her skin and closed his eyes, knowing he'd failed, when a shudder went through Ursula's body as her orgasm washed over her.

Relief flooded him at the same time as warm blood rushed into his mouth and down his throat. Had he been able to speak, he would have thanked her for having saved him once more, but he couldn't let go of the breast he was sucking on. Her blood tasted rich and sweet. Perfect. And to take it from her breast had become one of his favorite places to drink. Right along with her inner thigh, where he could soak in her arousal at the same time as he fed from her.

"Oh, yes." She encouraged him now, her hand sliding to his nape to press him closer to her breast.

Oliver knew how much she loved feeding him like this because it was something only he did. None of the leeches at the blood brothel she'd been imprisoned at for three long years had ever been allowed to take her blood from anywhere else than her neck or wrist.

With one last thrust, he came and flooded her tight channel with his seed. His entire body shook from the intensity of his climax. It took long moments before he could think clearly again and was able to retract his fangs from her breast. Gently he licked over the two small incisions, sealing them instantly. There would be no scars. His saliva guaranteed it.

Oliver dropped his head next to hers, breathing heavily.

"Wow. I love it when you do it like that."

He lifted his head to look at her. "How?"

"All out of control."

He shook his head. "It was close. I almost bit you before you climaxed. But I—"

She put a finger to his lips, stopping him from continuing. "Almost. I'll make sure it won't happen."

Oliver dropped his forehead to hers. "I thought it had gotten easier, but it hasn't. What if one day you won't come in time?"

"Then we'll deal with it. Together." She gave him a soft slap on his backside. "Besides, you can always make me come."

He chuckled. "That's what a guy likes to hear." He pressed a gentle kiss on her lips.

"It's time to go," she murmured back.

"I know."

2

Ursula fidgeted as she nervously watched the escalator that descended from the arrival level to the baggage claim area at San Francisco International Airport where she and Oliver were waiting. She turned to him.

"You know what to tell them, right?" she asked.

Oliver clasped her hand then led it to his lips, pressing a soft kiss on her knuckles. "Don't look so anxious! Your parents will wonder whether something is wrong."

She sighed. "Well, that's because something *is* wrong. I've been living in sin with you, and if they ever find out—"

"What are they gonna do? Force me to marry you?" He chuckled. "Guess what? That's what we're gonna do anyway."

"Still, there's no need to upset them."

"Upset them? I thought they liked me."

"They do," she hastened to assure him. "Though I'm sure they would have preferred if I married a nice Chinese boy instead."

Oliver grimaced. "Hey, two out of three ain't bad."

"Two out of what three?" she asked.

He lifted his fingers and started counting. "Good looking and great in bed." He shrugged.

Ursula shook her head and rolled her eyes. "Yeah, about the latter. I'm sure my parents wouldn't appreciate the fact that I shacked up with you for all these months while they thought I was living at the dorms at UC Berkeley."

"Shacking up with me? I'd hardly call it that." He gave her a soft smile, his eyes dropping to her lips and his head inching closer. "Actually, I preferred it when you called it 'living in sin.' It's got a much nicer ring to it."

Ursula nudged him in the ribs. "You're terrible. I wish you'd take this seriously."

"You mean the 'living in sin' part? I take it very seriously. And I thought you liked it. I did. Immensely."

She felt her entire body flush with heat. He could do that to her with the way he gazed into her eyes, his mouth parting, and his fangs starting to elongate as a sign of his desire for her.

"Oliver, your fangs," she whispered under her breath.

He closed his mouth instantly and swallowed. "See what you do to me. You start talking about sin, and I turn all primal."

She couldn't help but smile. "Maybe then it's a good thing we're getting married. At least then it won't be considered a sin anymore."

Oliver bent to her, placing a soft kiss near her ear. "I don't care what it's called. It won't change the way I feel about you. Nor the fact that the next week will be pure torture for me."

She lifted her eyes to meet his look. "It's the only way we can hide from my parents what's been going on the last few months."

He let out a resigned sigh.

"Let's go over the story again, just so we don't trip ourselves up," she suggested and cast another look up the escalator as more people started to descend.

"Okay," Oliver agreed. "You've been living at the dorms, but in order to prepare for the wedding, you moved into the guestroom in my parents' house today, and your parents will be staying in my room, while I move in with Samson until the wedding." He shoved a hand through his unruly dark hair. "I hope I can remember to call Quinn

Dad. At least Rose I can still call Rose."

"Why?"

"Well, she's not my mother. I'm only related to Quinn as my sire. So, we should tell your parents that Rose is my stepmother. That way, I won't trip myself up when I address her as Rose."

Panic gripped Ursula. Last-minute changes to an established plan always spelled disaster. "Did you talk to Quinn and Rose about that already?"

Oliver squeezed her hand. "Don't worry about it. I discussed it with them and also with Blake."

Relieved, Ursula let out a breath. "Okay. And Blake knows what to say and do?"

Blake, who was human and Rose and Quinn's fourth great-grandson, could be a goofball, but she hoped that he would stick to the plan they'd put together and help them fool her parents that the Ralston-Haverford-Bond family—Quinn Ralston, Rose Haverford, Blake Bond, and Oliver, who had taken Quinn's last name after his turning—was a typical American family and didn't consist of three vampires and a human.

"Blake will be on his best behavior. I promise you that."

Ursula rolled her eyes. "Right."

"I'll keep him in line. He's still scared shitless that I'll bite him again. So, don't worry about him."

She smiled at him softly. "But that's a bluff. I know you won't bite him. You don't even like his blood."

Oliver pulled her closer, turning her into his body. "That's because you spoiled me with yours. Everything else tastes like battery acid to me." He inhaled deeply. "Oh God, I can smell your blood now."

Ursula shivered as he placed his lips on her neck and kissed her gently. "You've gotta stop. People are looking at us."

"You're killing me, baby. I hope you know what you're asking of me to stay out of your bed for an entire week." He lifted his head, and their gazes locked. The rim of his irises shimmered golden, a sign that his vampire side was emerging.

She caressed his cheek. "I know, my love. I'll make it up to you later."

"How?" he asked, his voice a husky murmur.

She chuckled quietly. "Since when don't you have any imagination?" She let her hand slide to his neck and scratched her fingernails against it, feeling how his skin turned to gooseflesh underneath her touch.

Oliver groaned. "I can't wait. After this evening, I've gotten the taste for a lot more." His eyes seemed to penetrate her. "To suckle from your breast was—"

"Oh, no!" she interrupted him in panic. She'd just remembered something. "My bra!"

He looked at her, startled. "What's with your bra?"

She grabbed his arm. "It's still in your bedroom! I didn't pick it up. Where did it go? Did you pick it up when we moved the boxes with my stuff to the guestroom?"

He shook his head. "I don't think so. I didn't notice it anywhere."

Ursula's pulse raced. "Oh God, my mother is gonna find it and then she'll know."

"Is it really gonna be such a problem?" he asked softly.

"Yes!"

Oliver sighed and pulled his cell from his pocket. "Fine. I'll take care of it."

"How?"

He unlocked his cell and started typing. "I'll text Blake to look for it."

"Blake?" Embarrassment swept through her. "You can't have Blake look for my bra!"

Oliver tilted his head to the side. "Rose went out shopping, so she can't do it. So if you don't want your mother to find it in my room, then it's going to have to be Blake."

Ursula ground her teeth. "Oh, crap!" Her gaze drifted to a crowd of people coming down the escalator.

He chuckled. "I'm assuming that's a 'yes'?"

She nodded reluctantly and glanced at him as he pressed "send" on his cell phone before slipping it back into his pocket. She'd had no choice, because she'd just spotted her parents at the top of the escalator. There was no time to come up with another solution.

"They're here!"

From the top of the escalator, her parents descended, their eyes scanning the waiting area below. Her mother, a petite woman with impeccable taste and style, wore a costume that looked like it was designed by Chanel, though Ursula knew that her mother would never spend that kind of money on clothes. She was a veritable bargain hunter, and Ursula was sure that she hadn't spent more than a hundred dollars for her entire outfit including her shoes and her fancy handbag.

Involuntarily, Ursula had to smile. Her mother would be shocked if she found out how much money Oliver's family was spending on this wedding. Her parents were well off, with her father earning an exceptionally large salary as a high-level diplomat for the Chinese embassy in Washington D.C., so there was no need for her mother to be frugal, but it was so ingrained in her that she just couldn't help herself. It seemed almost like a sport to her.

Ursula waved as she caught her father's eye. He beamed at her, then touched his wife's arm to point to where Ursula and Oliver stood waiting. Excitedly, her mother waved back, but Ursula's gaze wandered back to her father. It seemed as if he'd lost weight. His face looked paler than usual too. She shook her head. The neon lights weren't flattering for anybody's skin tone. It had to be an optical illusion or the fact that he was tired from the flight.

When her parents reached the bottom steps of the escalator and stepped off it, Ursula flung herself into their arms, reaching around them both and hugging them tightly.

"I missed you!" she said, pushing back the tears.

"We missed you too, Wei Ling," her father said, calling her by her Chinese name as he did so often.

"You're going to squash your mother if you hold on any tighter," Oliver said from behind her and put a hand on her shoulder.

Ursula stepped out of their embrace, wiping away a tear that had escaped her eye.

Oliver moved to her side and stretched out his hand toward her mother first. "It's very nice to see you again, Mrs. Tseng."

Her mother took his hand and shook it, then put her other hand over it to clasp it. "Young man, maybe it's time to stop calling me Mrs. Tseng. My name is Hui Lian," she said with the Chinese accent that even after two decades in the US had not diminished.

Oliver grinned. "I'd like that very much, Hui Lian." Then he turned to her father and shook his outstretched hand. "It's good to see you, sir."

"Call me Yao Bang. And considering you're stealing my only daughter from me, I'm rather happy to see you too. It's good to know she'll be in good hands."

Her parents exchanged a look.

All of a sudden, a strange sense of unease slithered down Ursula's back like a snake. A cold shiver followed.

"Well, let's get your luggage so we can get you home," Oliver announced and motioned toward the carousels.

* * * *

He shouldn't even be on the arrival level at San Francisco International Airport, but he'd followed a particularly tasty smelling woman who'd made her way down there from the departure level where he'd been about to check in for the red-eye to New York. When he'd smelled her enticing blood, he'd decided to get one last *snack* before his flight and had followed her.

He was done with San Francisco. After he'd been captured by people from Scanguards, the self-appointed police force and self-righteous group of vampires who thought themselves above everybody else, they'd incarcerated him and others like him for several months and forced them to undergo a detox program. Rehab they'd called it!

He and the other vampires had been addicted to special blood from Chinese blood whores that a blood brothel in Hunter's Point had provided. But one day the blood brothel had disappeared and shortly afterwards, Scanguards had killed its owner and the guards, taken the girls away, and rounded up the clients. To make them undergo treatment!

What a crock of shit that was! He knew that now. And the reason he knew it was because there at one of the luggage carousels, one of Scanguards so-called bodyguards stood, his arm around one of the blood whores he recognized. And from the fragments of conversation he picked up, he realized that this vampire, who he'd met before and whose name was Oliver, if he wasn't mistaken, was getting married to this blood whore.

Hadn't the people from Scanguards said that all the blood whores had been sent home? Clearly, they'd dished up a bunch of lies, trying to pacify him and the other addicts, while behind their backs they were keeping the blood whores for themselves.

His mouth salivated as the girl's smell drifted to him. He pulled the scent deep into his lungs. Instantly, his sense memory projected vivid images into his mind. He'd never experienced anything as exhilarating as the blood of these women. It was special, and it acted like a drug to a vampire. He'd experienced that drug and had never felt a high as powerful as when he'd been suckling on the neck of one of the blood whores.

His gut clenched as the same hunger resurfaced now. He'd thought he was clean, but it appeared rehab hadn't worked. He wanted the drugged blood of this woman. And it wasn't fair that the people from Scanguards kept this treat for themselves. What hypocrites! They'd made him and the others suffer through the symptoms of withdrawal while they gorged themselves on the delicious blood.

The woman he'd followed earlier was forgotten, as was his flight to New York. He wasn't leaving. No, he would stay and get his fair share. The Chinese girl on Oliver's arm would become his meal. He would show those arrogant men from Scanguards that he had just as much a right to this blood as they.

He would show Oliver that he had no right to monopolize her.

3

Oliver set the two suitcases down inside his room and turned around, motioning his soon-to-be in-laws to enter.

"I hope you'll be comfortable here."

Ursula's parents stepped into the room and let their eyes roam, while Ursula walked in behind them, her eyes equally examining the bedroom, though he was sure she was searching for her bra. Blake had not texted him back, therefore it was possible that he'd either not received the text instructing him to search for the bra or was out.

"We could have easily stayed at a hotel," Ursula's mother said. "There was no need to go through all this trouble."

"No trouble at all," he replied quickly. "My parents thought it would be best if you two took my room. And Ursula will be in the guestroom. That way, you're all together, which makes it much easier for all the wedding preparations."

Ursula's father looked at his daughter. "You're staying in this house, Wei Ling?"

"Uh, yes, Dad, but only because of the preparations for the wedding. I just moved my stuff from the dorms this morning. It would be such a trek each day to get over the bridge from Berkeley and back. I would waste too much time, and there's so much to do," Ursula replied hastily.

"I don't think it's appropriate for you to stay in the same house as

Oliver. It's bad luck," her mother cut in and turned toward Oliver. "I'm sorry, Oliver, but we can't do that. We can move to a hotel with Ursula. Somewhere central."

Oliver took a steadying breath. Ursula had warned him that her parents were old-fashioned as well as superstitious. "It's really not an issue. I won't be staying here this week. I'm going to stay at my boss's house until the wedding."

Mrs. Tseng raised an eyebrow. "Your boss's house? That's very generous of him to let you stay. Well, then, of course . . . " She exchanged a look with her husband.

Ursula's father nodded. "Thank you, Oliver. That's very thoughtful of you. This looks very comfortable and spacious."

Relieved, Oliver pointed to a door. "You have your own bathroom and sitting area so you can relax. But feel free to use any part of the house. I'll show you around once you've had a chance to freshen up."

His sensitive hearing picked up the sound of footsteps on the stairs. Then a human smell drifted to him. He recognized the smell immediately. A moment later, Blake popped his head through the door.

"Hey!" he said.

"Hui Lian, Yao Bang, meet my half-brother, Blake. Blake, these are Ursula's parents, Mr. and Mrs. Tseng."

Blake let a big smile spread over his face as he walked toward them and shook their hands. "So nice to finally meet you. Ursula talks about you day and night."

"Day and *night*?" her father repeated, aiming a stern look in Ursula's direction.

Crap! Oliver thought. Leave it to Blake to say something that could get them in trouble. "What Blake means is Ursula speaks of you whenever she visits. You know, during the day."

Oliver felt sweat build on his nape. He tossed a displeased glance at Blake who shrugged, while Ursula's parents looked at their daughter.

"Yes, I told you, Dad. Oliver's family invites me over for dinner quite often," Ursula added and smiled.

Well, it wasn't entirely a lie, only that Ursula had become *Oliver's* favorite dinner and that after being invited to stay for the first time, she'd never left. But then, those were only minor details, albeit details they had to keep from her parents. Together with the other minor detail they had to hide: the fact that they were guests in a vampire household, and that their daughter was marrying a vampire.

What the hell had he been thinking? This would never work! Not his union with Ursula. No, they would be perfect together, but keeping the secret about what he was from her parents.

"When will we meet your parents, Oliver?" Ursula's father suddenly asked.

"They should be back any minute. I believe Rose had some shopping to do," Oliver replied, glad that the subject had turned to something less precarious than sleeping arrangements and how much time Ursula spent at his house.

"Rose? You call your mother by her first name?" Yao Bang asked in surprise.

"Well, she's my stepmother, so I've always called her Rose instead of Mom."

"Ah," Ursula's mother interrupted. "So, Rose is your mother then, Blake?"

"Yes, but, uh, well, since Oliver always called her Rose when we grew up, I call her Rose too."

Oliver turned so Ursula's parents couldn't see his face and rolled his eyes at Blake. Did he have to change the rules of the game? They'd expressly discussed who would call whom what. And now Blake threw a wrench into the whole machinery. Soon, this would blow up in their faces.

"Uh, I see," Mr. Tseng commented. "Well, as long as you all get on." Then he turned to peruse the room once more, his wife doing the same.

She walked closer to the bed and placed her handbag onto it.

"Oh, dear!" Mrs. Tseng suddenly said with a start and looked in the direction of his nightstand. Oliver followed her gaze, but Ursula's father was blocking his view.

Oliver turned to Ursula next to him, catching her panicked look, while he heard how her heartbeat accelerated. Clearly, she was thinking the same as he was: his mother had spotted Ursula's bra on the floor.

He had no choice now. He had to wipe her parents' memories to make sure that they never remembered seeing Ursula's incriminating underwear in his bedroom. He took a deep breath when he felt Blake's hand on his shoulder. Instantly he turned to him. His half-brother gave a slight shake with his head and dropped his gaze. Oliver followed it to Blake's jeans pocket. A little bit of black lace peeked from it. He grinned and shoved it down with his hand, making it disappear from Oliver's view.

Oliver mouthed a silent "thank you" to him and turned back to his future in-laws. If Mrs. Tseng hadn't found the bra, then what was she looking at?

With trepidation, Oliver took a few steps to walk around Mr. Tseng and saw what Mrs. Tseng was finding so offensive.

He had to stifle a laugh when he finally set eyes on the offending item. There, between his nightstand and the bed frame, one of his boxer briefs had gotten caught and hung suspended between the two pieces of furniture.

"I'm so sorry," he said hastily, grabbed the item and balled it up in his fist, then attempted to shove it in his jacket pocket.

"Maybe it was too inconvenient to get you to give up your room after all. We really shouldn't have imposed," her mother said.

"No, no. You're not imposing at all. I'm sorry. I guess I was in a hurry today."

Yeah, he sure had been in a hurry—in a hurry to make love to Ursula one more time before he was forced to move out of the house until the wedding. When he'd gotten dressed after they'd made love, he'd been in such a daze that he hadn't found his boxer briefs instantly and simply grabbed a new pair from his chest of drawers.

When he heard sounds behind him, he sighed in relief. The cavalry had arrived.

"Well, it looks like our guests are here," Quinn said from the door as he walked in, his wife Rose on his heels.

"I'm so sorry we weren't here to greet you," Rose instantly apologized and stretched her hand out to Ursula's mother.

"This is Rose, my stepmother, and this is Quinn, my father," Oliver introduced them. "Dad, Rose, these are Hui Lian and Yao Bang Tseng."

He watched as the faces of Ursula's parents turned to surprise while they shook hands and exchanged greetings with Rose and Quinn.

"You both seem so young," Ursula's mother said finally. Mr. Tseng nodded in agreement.

"Good genes," Quinn replied with a broad smile on his face.

"We get that all the time!" Rose chirped with a soft laugh and exchanged a loving look with her blood-bonded mate. "We were practically kids when we met. We got married when we were very young."

Oliver swept a quick gaze over Quinn and Rose. Both didn't only look like they were in their mid-twenties, they also looked nothing like him or Blake. While both he and Blake were dark haired, their supposed parents were both blond and had fair skin. There was no family resemblance among the four of them and rightly so. Quinn had sired Oliver with his blood and turned him into a vampire when he lay dying after a horrific car accident, and Blake, though he was their blood relative, hadn't retained any of Rose's and Quinn's fair looks. Blake was six generations removed from them, and they were in fact his fourth great-grandparents.

"I hope you'll both be comfortable here," Quinn continued.

"We didn't really want to put Oliver out by taking over his room," Ursula's father replied, motioning to his surroundings. "But thank you very much. I'm sure we'll be very comfortable here."

"Excellent!" Quinn agreed.

"Once you've unpacked and freshened up, why don't you come downstairs, and I'll show you around?" Rose offered. "It'll be chaotic in the next few days with preparing for the wedding, so I've had the kitchen stocked with everything you might need, and rather than have regular sit-down lunches and dinners, I figured everybody should just help themselves to anything they want. Don't you think so too?" She smiled at Mrs. Tseng.

Ursula's mother looked at her somewhat stunned, but then nodded.

Rose smiled. They'd agreed on this arrangement when discussing how to hide the fact from the Tsengs that neither Rose, Quinn, nor Oliver consumed any food. "It'll be so much easier considering we'll all have different schedules. What with the tent being built, the last-minute fittings for the dress, and whatever else comes up."

"A tent?" Ursula's father suddenly asked. "What for?"

Quinn stepped forward and put his arm around Mr. Tseng's shoulder. "I'll show you." He led him to the window and pointed to the garden below. "We'll have a large tent erected that will cover the entire backyard. The ceremony and reception will take place there."

Oliver watched as Mrs. Tseng stepped next to her husband. "Oh, that sounds nice."

Ursula nudged closer to Oliver, and he instantly pulled her against him, stealing a kiss while her parents looked out the window.

"It'll be perfect," he whispered into her ear, gently nibbling on her earlobe. "And afterwards, I'll make you mine forever."

4

He'd been watching the house half the night until Oliver emerged and left on foot shortly past two o'clock. He was alone. The blood whore wasn't with him. She was still inside the house, together with her parents and two other vampires, as well as a human male.

He waited until Oliver had completely disappeared from his view before leaving his hiding place across the street and approaching the house.

It would take some planning to get to the girl, since she was still surrounded by too many people, two of which were vampires. Had they all been human, he would simply walk into the house now and snatch her. The humans would turn into collateral damage. However, the two vampires could be trouble.

But he wasn't giving up easily. He'd continue to observe and find a weak spot. Like a tiger, he would lie in wait and watch his prey until an opportunity presented itself. Then he'd make his move and steal the blood whore right from under their noses. If the vampires who ran Scanguards thought they could put up rules for others but not live by them themselves, then he'd show them what he thought of that.

His gaze wandered to the windows on the upper floors. Some of them were still illuminated. He stood still and watched. Waited. He knew how to do that, how to stand silently without moving for hours. How to barely breathe so as not to make a sound. How to remain almost invisible. How to blend in.

Inside him, his hunger grew. Though it was impossible, he thought he could smell the blood whore's blood from where he stood in the shadows of a lush tree. Yes, he'd missed that smell, that taste. He'd missed it while he'd been in rehab. While this crazy psychiatrist Dr. Drake had blathered about restraint and willpower as they'd sat around in groups to talk about how they *felt* about their addiction. Oh, he'd hated those sessions! But he'd played along because he knew if he didn't, they'd never release him. It had taken a long time. Longer than for many of the other vampires. He'd been among the last group to be released from the underground cells at Scanguards, which had turned into a clandestine treatment center complete with daily visits by Dr. Drake and his hot little assistant with the enormous rack.

Shame that she was a vampire. Had she been human, he would have dug his fangs into her tits first chance he got. Instead, the prisoners had been fed bottled blood. Cold, lifeless blood. He'd hated that too. But again, he'd played along. All so they would release him.

And while he'd been suffering in his cell, fighting against his hunger for that special blood, fighting his urge to lash out at his captors, Oliver had been gorging himself on one of the blood whores. Well, not for much longer. Soon, she would be his.

I'm coming for you, *Ursula*.

* * * *

Oliver greeted Delilah, Samson's wife, who opened the door for him.

"So we've got you back for a week," she said smilingly and kissed him on the cheek.

Behind her, Isabelle staggered into the hallway before falling onto her butt, chuckling.

"Wow!" Oliver exclaimed and walked toward the toddler. "She's walking!"

"Yes, she started last week, and every day she gets more secure on her two feet. I think she might be able to walk at your wedding."

He stretched his arms toward Isabelle and lifted her up. "You mean she could be our little flower girl?"

"Just in case, I bought her a cute pink dress so she's got something appropriate to wear. But don't tell Ursula yet, because I don't know whether she'll be walking well enough by then." She stroked her hand over Isabelle's dark hair. "I had no idea that hybrids grew up so fast."

Isabelle beamed at her, flashing her tiny fangs.

"Oh, no, Isabelle! What did we talk about? No showing of fangs! Just like we practiced. There'll be a lot of humans around this week, and we don't want you to expose us, do we?"

Isabelle dropped her lids and closed her mouth, clearly understanding her mother's words.

"Now try again," Delilah encouraged her.

The toddler parted her lips and flashed her mother another grin. This time no fangs showed.

"Perfect." Delilah kissed her on the cheek and Isabelle reached her arms out to her.

Oliver released her and handed her over to her mother. "I'm sure she'll do perfectly fine." Then he changed the subject. "So, is Samson home or is he at headquarters?"

Delilah motioned to the back of the house. "He's in his private office. Drake is here. And so are Gabriel and Zane. Samson said to join them when you arrive."

"Thanks." He turned toward the long wood-paneled corridor leading to the back of the house.

"Oh, and Oliver," Delilah called after him, "I prepared the newly renovated guestroom in the attic for you. That way you won't get woken by Isabelle."

He looked over his shoulder. "Thanks, Delilah. Hope it wasn't too much trouble."

She made a dismissive gesture with her hand. "No trouble. We love having you here. Samson misses you."

In many ways, he missed Samson too. For over three years, when he'd still been human, he'd worked for the owner of Scanguards as his personal assistant. He'd been his eyes and ears during the day, watching out for him while he slept, trading shifts with Carl, his vampire butler. Oliver sighed heavily. He missed Carl. They'd been friends despite the fact that they couldn't have been more different. But Carl was gone.

Oliver pushed away the sad thoughts and knocked at the door to Samson's study.

"Come!" Samson's voice came from the inside.

He turned the knob and opened the door, then closed it behind him. Samson sat at his massive desk, while Dr. Drake, Gabriel, and Zane lounged on the sofa and the comfortable armchair.

"Hey, Oliver, you're just in time. Dr. Drake just arrived to give us an update," Samson greeted him and motioned him to sit.

With his short black hair, his hazel eyes, and an imposing over-six-foot frame, Samson was every inch the boss. He was the founder of Scanguards, the national security company that provided bodyguards to celebrities, politicians, and other wealthy individuals and organizations who could afford their services.

Opposite him, Dr. Drake, the only vampire psychiatrist—and one of the only two vampires trained as medical professionals in San Francisco—looked scrawny and lanky. Oliver had always found him an odd sort, though Samson and several others at Scanguards had used his services at one time or another.

"Great!" Oliver took a seat on the couch next to Zane. "Hey, guys!"

"Hey!" Zane ground out, clearly not happy to be in the same room as Drake.

He'd once been forced to attend a session with the psychiatrist and apparently not enjoyed it. Not that Oliver could blame the bald vampire. Zane wasn't one for *soft* things, emotions and the like. He was a lean, mean fighting machine, even though Oliver had seen glimpses of a softer side inside him when he'd first met his mate, Portia, a young hybrid. But at the moment, none of that softness was apparent. Zane looked as if he wanted to kill somebody.

"I think it was too early to let them go," Zane now bit out, looking at Gabriel for reinforcement.

Gabriel stroked his chin with his hand, contemplating his answer, then pushed a strand of dark hair, which had come loose from his ponytail, behind his ear. Oliver couldn't help but stare at the large scar that ran from his ear to his chin, a souvenir from the time when he'd been human. While the scar was ugly, there was something intriguing about Gabriel that made him an imposing figure who could drive fear into anybody.

"Dr. Drake gave everybody the all clear," Gabriel replied.

"What's going on?" Oliver asked, tossing a questioning look at his colleagues.

Dr. Drake sat up straighter. "As I was starting to elaborate, we terminated the rehab program. Scanguards did a fabulous job at rounding up all former clients of the blood brothel and bringing them in."

Zane snorted, his boots scratching loudly against the wooden floor. "I don't need you to tell me that we've done a good job."

Samson gave Zane a reprimanding look. "Let him talk."

The bald vampire leaned back and folded his arms over his chest. Oh yeah, Oliver could tell Zane was pissed. And he wasn't one to sugarcoat his opinions. If he didn't like something, he'd let you know. He and Zane had butted heads more than once. Nevertheless, he liked the guy. Zane's gut feeling was better than anybody else's. And in a fight, he was lethal.

Drake cleared his throat. "Well. Some of the patients were doing better than others. I believe it was a matter of willpower and motivation. Some responded to positive reinforcement better, and those were the ones we released a few weeks ago. I understand that Scanguards is still keeping an eye on them?"

Samson nodded and motioned to Gabriel.

"That's right," Gabriel answered. "But there has been no erratic behavior. All of them seemed to have integrated well again."

Drake nodded. "Good, good. And with the drug, so to speak, out of their reach, it's certainly made things easier."

The drug. Yes, the blood of all the Chinese women who'd been held at the blood brothel was indeed a drug to vampires. Highly addictive, utterly delicious, and producing a high. Oliver could only imagine it. He'd never gotten high from Ursula's blood, because they were taking precautions. He only bit her after she'd climaxed, because an orgasm diluted the potency of the blood for a short time.

"Yes, they're all back at home. All but Ursula," Oliver said almost to himself.

"Oh, I almost forgot," the doctor said. "Congratulations on your upcoming wedding!"

"Thank you!"

"Can we get on with business?" Zane interrupted.

Drake looked as if he wanted to roll his eyes but refrained from doing so. "Last night we released the remaining vampires in our care. They've proven to us that they are strong enough to fight the temptation and have conquered their addiction. They're all clean now. I don't believe we'll have any more problems with regards to this issue."

"Proven how?" Zane shot back. "By sitting in some stupid group sessions, babbling about how they felt?"

Drake narrowed his eyes. "Yes, by talking about their feelings, which is a proven psychological tool."

"I'll give you a tool. A stake is a tool," Zane muttered under his breath.

Samson rose. "You know as well as I do that we couldn't simply kill those men because of their addiction. We had to help them." His gaze drifted to Oliver, and Oliver instinctively knew what his boss was thinking of. Samson had helped him when he'd been in the gutter, when he'd been an addict and running with a bad crowd. He'd given him a chance to lead a productive life instead.

"I have to agree with Samson. We had to help them," Oliver added. "They are our fellow vampires. If we don't help them, who will?"

If Samson hadn't helped him and given him a job, he wouldn't be here now. And if Quinn hadn't saved his life by turning him into a vampire when he lay dying after a car crash, he would have never known what love was.

Zane clenched his jaw. "I just hope it won't come and bite us in the ass one day."

Oliver caught Zane's gaze and for a moment, their eyes locked. Was Zane's concern valid?

5

"You have *four* bridesmaids?" Her mother nearly gasped at the revelation.

"Yes," Ursula replied, using her fingers to elaborate. "There's Portia, who's married to Zane. She's a little younger than I. Then Nina who's married to Amaury. And Maya, Gabriel's wife. Plus Lauren. She's a good friend of Portia's and I like her a lot."

Still, her mother kept shaking her head. "No, no. That won't work."

"But, Mom, those are my friends. Besides, they've already got their dresses." Ursula looked across the table to her father, who had his head buried in his newspaper. He dropped it slightly and shrugged. "Dad," she pleaded.

"That's your mother's domain. You know I don't get involved in women's business."

The frown on her mother's forehead deepened as she rose from the breakfast table. "Don't you have any other friends? Anybody from college?"

"What's wrong with those friends? You haven't even met them yet. How can you be against them?" Ursula felt herself get defensive. Her mother often had that effect on her.

"I'm not against your friends," she insisted and sighed heavily. "But you need more of them."

Ursula's forehead creased. "More?" She was perfectly fine with the friends she had. Besides, the only person she really wanted to spend time with was Oliver. But of course, he wasn't here. He had to stay at Samson's house during daytime.

Her mother stepped closer and gripped her chin, making her look up. "Have I taught you nothing about our culture when you grew up? You can't have four bridesmaids. Four means death. And you don't invite death to a wedding."

"Hui Lian, don't you think you're being a little overly dramatic?" her father suddenly interrupted.

Then it clicked for Ursula. Why she had forgotten that fundamental fact she didn't know. Maybe it was simply the stress of the wedding preparations that was getting to her.

"But you can't ask me to tell one of them that she can't be my bridesmaid. That wouldn't be fair. Dad, please help me here." All four of her friends were looking forward to being bridesmaids.

Her mother softly stroked over Ursula's hair. "Of course not, Wei Ling. That's why you'll have to find four more. We'll need eight bridesmaids. Eight will bring you luck."

Relieved, Ursula exhaled. "I guess I could ask Delilah and Yvette."

"Who are they?"

"Delilah is married to Samson. You'll meet him soon. He's Oliver's boss. And Yvette works for Scanguards too."

"So Yvette is one of the secretaries?"

Ursula shook her head, suppressing a laugh. If Yvette heard that, she'd have a fit. "No, Mom, she's a bodyguard like Oliver."

"A woman?"

She could firmly see the wheels in her mother's head turn.

"Well, maybe she's not the best choice then. We'll probably never find a dress for her."

Ursula pulled back. "What? Why not?"

"Well, if she's a bodyguard, you know . . . " Her mother hesitated and lowered her voice. "She's probably very butch. Isn't that what it's called? I mean, if she's a bodyguard."

Ursula shook her head in disbelief. "Oh my god! Just because she's a bodyguard doesn't mean she looks masculine. There's nothing butch about Yvette. She's one of the most feminine women I know."

Her father dropped his newspaper and folded it, a smirk on his face. Ursula met his gaze and had to grin when her father rolled his eyes, a gesture that luckily Ursula's mother didn't notice.

"Oh!" At least her mother had the decency to blush. "Well, in that case . . . But we still need two more to make it eight."

Sometimes Ursula really wondered how her mother could still hold on to all the prejudices she'd grown up with, while she'd lived in Washington D.C. for the past twenty years and had been exposed to a diverse population.

"Do you have any other friends you can ask?"

Ursula searched her mind. "I guess we could ask Rose. I'm sure she'll do it."

"Well, it's unusual to have one's future mother-in-law as a bridesmaid, but I guess we don't have much choice."

"Don't let Rose hear that. I don't want her to think we only asked her because we were in a jam." Luckily both Rose and Quinn were still asleep and would remain so for another few hours.

Her mother let out an outraged breath. "Wei Ling, you make me sound like I have no tact. Did you hear that, Yao Bang?" She glanced at her husband, who simply acknowledged her words with a smile, knowing that she didn't really expect an answer. "Of course, I won't say anything to Rose."

Ursula refrained from rolling her eyes. Instead, she contemplated who could become her eighth bridesmaid. She didn't know many women in San Francisco. She'd only attended a few classes since her escape from the blood brothel and had not really connected to anybody. Her life was with Oliver. Besides, the need to keep his secret had made her cautious about whom she invited into their home. She had to choose somebody who knew about vampires.

. . . or was a vampire herself. Vera.

"I know a very nice Chinese lady. I can ask her."

"A Chinese woman? That's wonderful. Who is she? Do we know her family?"

Ursula chuckled. "Mom, just because she's Chinese doesn't mean you know her or her family." It was highly unlikely considering Vera had been a vampire for some time. And she didn't exactly move in the same circles as her parents. Ursula was certain of that. Vera ran a high class brothel in Nob Hill, whereas her parents rubbed shoulders with other diplomats and government officials in Washington D.C. "There are hundreds of thousands of Chinese people living in San Francisco."

The sound of the doorbell startled her. She looked to the wall clock. Rarely anybody ever visited a vampire household this early. It was barely past ten in the morning.

She was about to get up to see who was visiting when she heard heavy footsteps coming down the stairs.

"Coming!" Blake called out to whoever had rung the bell.

A moment later, she heard the door open and another familiar voice greet him: Wesley, Haven's brother.

"Hey, hope I'm not too early, but you said the tent guys were starting early."

Their voices came closer and within a few seconds, both humans entered the kitchen. Well, technically Wesley was a witch, though his powers left much to be desired. According to what both Blake and Oliver had told her, Wesley had still not been able to gain all his witch powers back that he'd been robbed of shortly after his birth.

"Hey, morning, guys!" Blake greeted them, then pointed to Wesley. "This is Wesley Montgomery. Wes, these are Ursula's parents: Bang Tseng and Liliana Tseng. Did I get that right?"

Ursula cringed and shook her head, indicating to Blake that he'd just butchered her parents' names. "It's actually Yao Bang and Hui Lian."

Blake scratched his head, grinning unashamedly. "Oops! Well I knew it was something like *Bang Bang*." He made his hand into a gun, pretending to shoot. "That's kind of how I remember things. You know, associate the words with something familiar. Sorry. And *Liane*—so is that a diminutive of Lillian?"

Ursula rolled her eyes. Wordlessly, she mouthed, *stop it*, while swiping her index finger horizontally across her throat. She could always count on Blake to screw things up.

Meanwhile Wesley politely shook her parents' hands. "Nice to meet you, Mrs. Tseng, Mr. Tseng. I hope you had a good flight."

Her parents smiled at Wesley, clearly relieved not to have to listen to any further butchering of their names.

"Did I hear that the tent will be built this morning?" her father asked.

"Yes, that's why I figured I'd come and help out. To supervise the workers. Make sure they don't mess things up and break stuff," Wesley offered.

Her father turned to her. "Is Oliver not coming to help with that?"

"He can't. He's protecting a client today," Ursula answered quickly, pasting a regretful expression onto her face. "Last-minute booking. They couldn't find anybody else on such short notice. It's their busy season, Dad."

He raised an eyebrow. "Oh, I had no idea there were seasons for bodyguards."

"Oh yeah, totally!" Blake chimed in. "Whenever there are any political or big society events, we get a lot more bookings."

Her father gave Blake a scrutinizing look. "So you're a bodyguard too."

Blake nodded proudly. "Yes. I work for Scanguards too."

"Me too!" Wesley piped up, as if this were a competition. And between those two guys it generally was.

"Hmm, so if you two are bodyguards at Scanguards, why is it that Oliver had to take a booking when he should be taking care of these things, rather than one of you helping with the wedding arrangements?"

"Uh," Blake mumbled.

"Neither Blake nor Wesley are fully trained yet," Ursula said quickly. "They don't have all their certifications yet, so they're not allowed to protect a client on their own."

The explanation seemed to satisfy her father. "Well, good, then."

Another ring of the doorbell interrupted them.

"That'll be the tent guys. I'll let them in," Blake announced.

As he walked back into the hallway, Wesley on his heels, Ursula felt her mother's hand on her arm. She turned to her.

"We'll need to somehow get dresses for the extra four bridesmaids," her mother announced, looking at the list in her hands.

"I'll first have to talk to them."

"Good. Call them and while you're talking to them, ask them for their dress size, and then we'll need to go shopping. Do you have a local seamstress who can help us make alterations if we need to?"

Her mother was a veritable waterfall of questions.

"And when we've found the right dresses, they can meet us for the fitting."

"But can't we just get the dresses, bring them here, and then have everybody try them on and then get a seamstress to make the alterations here?" Ursula suggested. Having Yvette, Rose, and Vera meet them for a fitting during the day would be impossible. As vampires, they had to avoid daylight. Only the humans and the hybrids would be able to do a daytime fitting.

"That's too complicated. We'll have to do it right at the shop."

"But that won't work."

"Why not?"

Ursula scrambled for an excuse. "Well, they work during the day. They can't take time off."

"Rose works?" Her mother's head motioned to the ceiling. "But she's still asleep."

"Uh." Panic raced through Ursula. "Well, she starts a little later. I'm sure we can do something one evening."

Her mother gave her a displeased look. "You're making this all very difficult, Wei Ling! I'm just trying to help you."

"I know, Mom," she said quickly in order not to upset her. "I really appreciate it."

"Well, then, let's not waste any more time."

Ursula already sensed how this week would turn out: stressful, exhausting, and chaotic. And she dreaded every single minute of it, knowing that Oliver wouldn't be around much. Maybe pretending to her parents that she and Oliver didn't have an intimate relationship hadn't been such a good idea after all. Maybe she should have just come out with it at the beginning. Her parents would have been upset at first, but at least Oliver would have been able to stay at the house. And she would have a shoulder to lean on and arms around her to wipe away the stress of planning a wedding.

6

The door to the tradesmen entrance which opened to a narrow path leading along Quinn's house stood open, and two men were carrying heavy metal rods through the walkway.

The moment the sun had set, Oliver had walked the short distance from Samson's Nob Hill house to Quinn's mansion in Russian Hill. He'd not taken the car to Samson's, because there was no extra parking in the garage, and parking on the streets of Nob Hill was virtually impossible.

Oliver followed the workers through the narrow walkway that led into the garden, curious to see how far they'd gotten.

When he reached the garden, he looked around. Several men were busy, connecting metal rods to build a scaffold that would eventually be draped with huge canvas panels to create a tent that covered the entire backyard and connected seamlessly to the back of the house and its back entrance. A sliver of it would also drape around the other side of the house to lead to the French doors in the living room so that the guests wouldn't have to trek through the kitchen or the dirty tradesmen entrance to get to the tent.

Things seemed to be moving at a swift pace, but Oliver knew it would take a good two days until the tent was operable. Only then could other things be brought in, like tables, chairs and decorations.

Oliver turned away from the workers and walked through the open door into the kitchen.

Wesley stood over the kitchen counter, munching on a sandwich.

"Hey!" Oliver greeted him.

The wannabe witch lifted his hand in greeting, his mouth too full to speak.

"Where is everybody?"

Wesley swallowed before he answered. "I suppose with 'everybody' you mean Ursula?"

Was he indeed that transparent? At any other time he would have denied it, but he missed the woman who would soon be his wife and his mate, and he couldn't care less whether Wesley wanted to tease him about it.

"So? Where is she?"

"Out shopping with her mother."

"Do you know when they'll be back?"

Wesley shrugged. "I heard something about bridesmaid's dresses. That's when I tuned out."

"And Ursula's father?"

"Probably still upstairs. He wanted to lie down and rest. I think the whole racket down here seems to have tired him out." Wes set down his half-eaten sandwich and walked to the door that led into the hallway, peered outside for a moment, then closed it again and turned back. "So while we're alone, I wanted to ask you for a favor."

Oliver lifted an eyebrow, always suspicious when Wesley wanted something because whatever it was, it generally led to a minor disaster. "What kind of favor?"

Wesley rubbed his neck. "Well, you heard about the puppies, right?"

"Haven's Labrador puppies that you once turned into piglets with your magic?"

A sheepish grin spread over Wesley's face. "Yeah, it's just, I've been trying to turn them back into dogs, but it hasn't worked."

Surprised, Oliver couldn't suppress the chuckle that built in his chest. "Are you telling me that they are still pigs?"

"Haven is none too happy about it either. So, I hit the books and came across this spell that should work. Only thing is, I need a few drops of vampire blood to—"

"No way!" Oliver interrupted. "Go hit up your brother!"

Wesley made a grimace. "He's already turned me down. So I figured maybe you'd wanna help out."

Oliver narrowed his eyes. "Is that why you volunteered to help out with the wedding preparations, so you can get me to give you some of my blood?"

Wesley huffed, outraged. "As if I would do that! I'm helping out because I want to. I thought we were friends."

"You're totally transparent, Wes!"

He shrugged. "So? Come on. It's just a few drops. I brought a little vial. You won't even feel it. It's just a pinprick. And it's all for the greater good. If I can't turn those pigs back into dogs, they'll eventually turn into bacon and sausage."

Oliver rolled his eyes. "Which I believe are the nicknames Blake gave them."

He knew Wes all too well. He would nag and be a total pest until he'd gotten what he wanted. It was better to get it over with. Besides, Wes was right. Giving him a few drops of vampire blood wouldn't hurt, nor would it be harmful to anybody. After all, vampire blood had great healing properties.

"Fine. But you owe me one and don't think I won't collect! Only a few drops. And it'll be the only time," he conceded.

Wesley beamed. "I swear!" He pulled a small glass vial just big enough for one fluid ounce from his pocket. "Here, just half-full is fine."

Still shaking his head, Oliver elongated his fangs, bringing them to full length. Instantly, he felt power surge through him, a result of his vampire side emerging. The lingering scent of Ursula drifted to his nostrils and cocooned him. If she were in the kitchen now, while his fangs were extended, he didn't think he could resist biting her. The bottled blood he'd consumed at Samson's had nourished him yet not truly satisfied him. The only thing that could truly satisfy his hunger was Ursula's blood and her body writhing beneath his.

"Uh, Oliver," Wesley prompted him, pulling him from his thoughts.

Swiftly he brought his thumb to his lips and pricked it with one of his fangs. He held the vial under his bleeding digit and let it drip into it, watching as the level quickly rose to midway.

"Oh, Oliver, you're here."

Oliver's head snapped to the door leading into the hallway. Ursula's father stood there, looking somewhat pale.

When their gazes met, Yao Bang's eyes widened in shock and disbelief. "Oh, no!" he pressed out. "That can't be!"

Oliver's forehead furrowed, while Wesley ground out low under his breath, "Your fangs!"

"Shit!" Oliver cursed, but it was too late.

He hadn't retracted his fangs, and his future father-in-law had seen them. He made a move toward him and noticed him shrink back toward the door. At the same time, Wesley snatched the open vial that Oliver still held in his hand.

Oliver tossed Wes an angry glare. Because of him, he'd exposed himself.

Wesley shrugged. "Wipe his memory then."

Yao Bang's mouth opened for a scream, but Oliver was on him before it could leave his throat, clamping his hand over his mouth and preventing him from escaping by clutching him to his body. At the same time, he reached out his mind to the older man and sent his thoughts to him.

You saw nothing. You came into the kitchen for a snack and saw me and Wesley making sandwiches. That's all you saw. You never saw my fangs. You never saw any blood.

Yao Bang's eyes went blank, the fear in them wiped away. Relieved, Oliver released him and stepped back.

"Oliver," Yao Bang murmured, before he staggered a few steps forward, reaching out his arms to grasp for support.

Oliver grabbed hold of him before he could fall, then felt him go slack in his arms. He was unconscious.

"Crap!"

"What did you do now?" Wesley asked.

"I didn't do anything!" Wiping somebody's memory didn't have that kind of effect on humans. Nobody had ever fainted after he'd wiped his memory. This was not right. Something had gone wrong. "Shit, shit, shit!" Ursula could never find out about this. "Call Maya! Now! Get her here as fast as she can. Tell her to take the side entrance so Ursula won't see her when she comes back."

Wesley pulled out his cell phone and dialed.

Oliver gently lowered his future father-in-law onto the ground and checked his vital signs, when his sensitive hearing picked up the opening of the front door. He inhaled sharply. Shit! Ursula and her mother were coming back. Panicked, he looked around the kitchen, wondering what to do.

"Why don't you bring all the dresses upstairs into my room, Wei Ling? I'll make some tea," Ursula's mother said from the hallway, her voice coming closer as she walked in the direction of the kitchen.

"Okay, Mom." He heard Ursula's reply, accompanied by footsteps on the stairs.

The kitchen door opened before Oliver could make a decision as to what to do with Yao Bang and how to explain his unconsciousness.

"Oh my god! Yao Bang!" Hui Lian said, running to where he lay on the floor. She stroked her hand over his head. Then her eyes shot to Oliver.

An inadequate excuse already sat on his lips, but he didn't get to utter it.

"We can't tell Ursula about this. Promise me." Her eyes pleaded with Oliver.

Surprised, Oliver pulled back. What did she know? Did she have an inkling that he was an immortal creature and knew what he'd done to her husband? But how?

"He has these fainting spells. The doctors think it's maybe anemia. But we didn't have time for more tests before the trip. Oh God, I hoped this wouldn't happen."

"Maya is on her way," Wesley interrupted.

"Maya?" Hui Lian asked, her eyebrows pulling together in confusion.

Oliver put a reassuring hand on her forearm. "She's a doctor. She'll check him out. He'll be fine." Relief washed through Oliver. Wiping Yao Bang's memory hadn't done this to him. He'd looked pale the moment he'd stepped into the kitchen. He'd probably been about to faint even if he hadn't seen Oliver's fangs. Still, Oliver felt responsible for what had happened.

"But we can't have Ursula see the doctor arrive. She'll be worried. She doesn't need this in the week she's getting married," her mother claimed.

"I'll distract her and keep her upstairs until Maya is gone again."

Hui Lian gave him a grateful smile. "Thank you so much. You're a good man."

For a moment their eyes locked, and for the first time, Oliver felt affection for Ursula's mother. She wanted only the best for her daughter and didn't want to destroy Ursula's happiness even if that meant keeping things from her. That's what they had in common. They would both keep secrets from Ursula if that meant she would be happy.

7

Ursula dropped the shopping bags on the floor of Oliver's room where her parents were staying and plopped onto the bed, kicking her shoes off in the process. All she wanted was to curl up into a ball and hide. She was exhausted and her nerves were strung so tightly, they would at this point snap at the slightest confrontation with anybody. Spending time shopping with her mother had been pure torture.

She stared up at the ceiling, sighing heavily, when the door opened. Immediately, she sat up. A smile formed on her lips when she set eyes on her visitor: Oliver.

"Hey, baby!" he greeted her and pulled her into his arms as he sat down on the bed.

Before she could even utter his name, his lips slid over hers and kissed her hungrily. While he'd always been a passionate kisser, Ursula felt that this kiss was more intense, more urgent than normal.

Oliver released her after several heart-pounding seconds.

"Looks like you missed me," she murmured against his lips. "Maybe we should be apart more often."

He growled low and deep. "Don't tease me. You know how I get when you play with me."

Ursula couldn't help but chuckle. She loved it when Oliver went all primal and possessive, when she should despise exactly that character trait in any man. Having been imprisoned for three years by crazy vampires should have scarred her forever so that she never wanted another man to act all possessive about her. But somehow when Oliver did it, it felt right. She wanted to be his. Forever.

Ursula ran her fingers along his neck and saw him visibly swallow when she brushed the artery that throbbed under his skin. "I wish we could start our new life together without all this fuss."

Oliver pulled back a few inches, looking at her quizzically. "What fuss?"

She made an all encompassing motion with her arm. "This. The wedding, the bridesmaids, the shopping, the flowers, everything."

"What? But we're doing this for you. I couldn't care less about a big wedding. Hell, if I had a say, I'd drag you to a secluded place with a big bed and blood-bond with you right now."

"I never wanted a big wedding either. But look at it now." She pointed to the window, indicating the large tent that was being built out there. "I'm not sure I'm prepared for all this."

"Then why are we doing it?" Oliver pushed a strand of her hair behind her ear, and she leaned into his palm, loving the way his touch comforted her.

"My parents. They want this. They think that if the wedding is perfect, the marriage will be perfect too." Particularly her mother believed that. Her father could have maybe been talked into something smaller and simpler, but even he had no chance once her mother had made up her mind.

"Our marriage will be perfect. I promise you that."

Ursula sighed. "But this wedding will be a disaster." She pointed to the shopping bags. "Do you know how many stores my mother dragged me to so we could find matching bridesmaid's dresses for the extra bridesmaids?"

"Extra bridesmaids? Are four not enough?"

"Four is a bad number in Chinese. It means death. So when Mom found out, she almost had a stroke! She insists that we have eight bridesmaids because eight is a lucky number."

Oliver shook his head. "She can't possibly believe that!"

Ursula rolled her eyes. "You don't know my mother! She's superstitious, controlling, a perfectionist and she drives me—"

"Don't, Ursula," he said softly, placing a finger on her lips. "Your mother only wants your best. She wants you to be happy and would do anything for you."

Ursula felt her eyebrows snap together. "How would you know that? You barely know her."

He smiled. "I just have a feeling. Trust me. She's doing this for you. Don't spoil it. I know you're stressed."

"Stressed is an understatement. I still have to get all the bridesmaids together for a fitting, and since half of them are vampires, we can't do it during the day. I'm running out of excuses why it will have to be at night. And then there's the cake, and Mom wants me to make wedding favors, and we still need to shop for some special table decorations. And then there are the flowers—"

"Stop, baby. I'll take care of some of those things for you."

"You would? Really?"

He pulled her against his chest. "Of course I will. It's my wedding too. How about I'll take care of the flowers and the cake? You won't have to worry about that at all."

Ursula threw her arms around his neck. "You're the best!"

Oliver grinned unashamedly and winked at her. "I'm the best at a lot of things. Do you want me to remind you?"

She gasped, pulled out of his arms, and shot a panicked look toward the door. "We can't! If my mother walks in here and sees us, she's going to give me a lecture on premarital sex, and I'm really not in the mood for that."

Oliver chuckled. "Your mother is busy in the kitchen. She won't disturb us for a while."

"You don't know her. Besides, it doesn't take forever to make tea. She'll be up here any moment." Ursula hopped off the bed and walked to the window. Below it, the tent was being built even though so far, it looked more like a scaffold used to paint a house rather than a tent. Several men still worked and floodlights had been installed to help them see in the dark. "When will the tent be up?"

She heard Oliver rise and walk to her. Then he pressed his body against her back und put his arm around her waist. "Maybe another day or two."

"Oliver?"

"Yes?"

"Do you sometimes think back to when we met?"

"All the time."

She turned her head halfway to look at him. "I'm glad it was you whose arms I collapsed in. You saved me."

Oliver smiled and shook his head. "No, *you* saved *me*. I was on a downward spiral. If I hadn't met you that night, I would have slid deeper, until one day I would have fallen prey to bloodlust. I was lucky to have found you."

She lifted herself on her tiptoes and turned in his arms. "I hope we'll always be as happy as now."

"We'll be even happier once we're blood-bonded. Then I'll be able to protect you better."

His words surprised her. "What do you mean?"

"I'll be able to sense when you're in danger because of the bond. And we'll be able to communicate telepathically."

She knew all about that aspect of the blood-bond. But some of his words made her ask, "Why would I be in danger?"

He shrugged. "Just saying. If anything ever happens, I'll know."

Ursula slapped his shoulder. "Don't spook me! Nothing will happen. I'm safe here."

He pressed a kiss to her forehead. "Yes, you're safe with me."

8

"It's too tight," Delilah complained.

She was one of eleven women assembled in the living room of Quinn and Rose's mansion, eight of whom were trying on their bridesmaid's dresses. Ursula tossed a glance in her mother's direction, who was assisting the seamstress in making some adjustments to Yvette's dress—or rather bossing the poor woman around.

Her mother hadn't heard Delilah over the din of voices in the room, which was currently off-limits to the men. In fact, Blake had been posted outside the door to make sure none of the workers carrying chairs and tables into the tent would accidentally step inside the room of scantily clad women.

"Let me help you," Ursula offered and approached Delilah.

Delilah, the pretty dark-haired woman with the green eyes, had a great figure, though she was a little rounder around her hips than some of the other women assembled. No wonder, she was the one who had borne a child a year earlier and seemingly had trouble getting rid of the last few pounds of pregnancy weight.

"Thank you, Ursula. I don't mean to be complicated, but if I zip it all the way up, I won't be able to breathe. I can't squeeze my boobs into this dress." Delilah glanced at her apologetically. "And I swear I didn't have any cookies in the last two weeks!"

Ursula chuckled and caught Maya's eye, who stood close and now approached. Maya let a long look wander over Delilah, then leaned in closer.

"I doubt it's the cookies, Delilah." Maya's eyes twinkled. "If you don't mind my saying so as your physician, it's generally not cookies that make your boobs swell."

Ursula noticed how Delilah sucked in a breath. "You don't think—" She stopped herself and ran her hand along her torso before resting it on her belly. "But, we've tried to be careful." Her cheeks colored prettily.

Ursula didn't have to be a brain surgeon to figure out what Maya was alluding to. "Are you saying Delilah is pregnant?" she whispered so nobody else in the room could hear them. Except maybe the other vampire females in the room, whose hearing was superior to that of humans: Rose, Yvette, Vera, as well as Portia and Lauren, who both were hybrids, half vampire, half human.

Maya smiled at Delilah. "I think you should come in for a test in the next few days. So we can be sure. I would love to study your pregnancy from beginning to end this time. Last time I only got the tail end of it."

"That is, if I'm really pregnant. I could well be just getting fat!" Delilah joked.

"With a man like Samson?" Maya looked at Ursula, and Ursula couldn't help herself but laugh.

"Maya is right. I mean I don't know Samson that well, but if he's anything like Oliver, then I'm surprised you only have one child so far." Shocked at her own words, Ursula slapped her hand over her mouth, then quickly scanned the room to see if her mother was close by. To her relief, she was still harassing the poor seamstress and giving her tips on how to do her job.

When she turned back to Maya and Delilah, both women were chuckling.

"Guess our Oliver has become quite a man," Delilah said, the affection for him shining through her words and eyes.

Ursula dropped her lids, suddenly embarrassed. "My parents don't know."

Ursula felt a hand on her forearm and looked up. Maya squeezed her arm briefly. "And they won't hear it from us."

"Thank you!"

"So, about the dress," Delilah started.

"Don't worry," Ursula said. "There should be enough inside seam so the seamstress can let it out to make it wide enough so you can breathe comfortably. Let me get her."

She walked to the seamstress, who knelt in front of Yvette to adjust the seam of her dress, and tapped her on the shoulder. "Ms. Petrochelli? Could you please help out my friend Delilah? Her dress is too tight. You'll need to let a little bit of the seam out."

"Too tight?" her mother interrupted, a panicked look on her face. "But you said she wore a size six. We bought her a size six."

"Yes, but it's just a little too tight." Ursula tried to calm her down, but it appeared it was already too late. Her mother had switched to panic mode and was already moving toward Delilah.

With a sigh, Ursula looked over her shoulder and watched how she stepped behind Delilah to try to zip her up. Then she gesticulated wildly and Ursula had to turn away. She couldn't watch. It would only make her stress about things even more.

"Your mother takes things too seriously," Yvette suddenly said, making Ursula look at her and smile.

"Don't all mothers?" She simply shrugged then let her eyes wander over Yvette's red dress. "You look great in this. It's totally your color."

Yvette smiled broadly. "I love it. I was just a little surprised that you chose red for the bridesmaid's dresses. Normally the bridesmaids get to wear some ghastly color like pink or orange, just so that they can't upstage the bride."

"Red means good luck at a Chinese wedding. The more red the better. Besides, with all of you except for Rose and Nina having dark hair, I figured it's a color that would look good on all of you." She chuckled. "And Rose and Nina can wear any color they want anyway."

Yvette laughed and winked at her. "Yes, blondes have all the fun."

Ursula had never seen her so lighthearted. As she joined in Yvette's laughter, she heard her mother's shocked gasp and turned, wondering what had gone wrong now.

Her mother stalked toward her, eyes wide, a dismayed look on her face. "Why didn't you tell me?"

Instinctively, Ursula backed away. Had somebody let it slip that she'd been living with Oliver? "Tell you what?" she managed to ask, trying to buy herself some time.

"About Oliver's date of birth!" Her mother's cheeks were flushed as her voice rose.

The other women fell silent and were suddenly all staring at them.

"Why didn't you tell me that he was born on the fourth of April?"

Ursula stared blankly at her mother. "What?" And who had even told her? She looked at the faces of her bridesmaids and saw Rose shrug and make a helpless gesture.

"Your mother asked so she could get a horoscope done as a surprise gift," Rose said apologetically.

"The fourth day of the fourth month, Ursula! How could you keep this from me?" her mother asked again.

That's when it finally clicked. It was a bad omen. With four meaning death in Chinese culture, for the groom to have two fours in his birth date spelled disaster. Ursula didn't believe in these superstitions, having grown up mostly in Western culture, but her mother was still too engrained in the old beliefs.

"It doesn't matter, Mom!" she answered.

"It matters! Have you no respect for your heritage? No belief in our culture?"

Ursula vaguely heard the chiming of the doorbell.

"I don't care when he was born. I love him!"

Her mother shook her head. "We have to change things. I'll have to get a horoscope done and see whether there's a day you can marry him that will counteract his date of birth. A day that'll be luckier than others."

"That's ridiculous! I'm not doing this! I'm getting married in two days, and that's that!" Ursula ran toward the door.

"Ursula!" her mother shouted.

"Mrs. Tseng," she heard Vera's voice. "Maybe I can help. I'm an expert in Chinese numerology."

Ursula pushed back the tears as she opened the door and stepped into the corridor. She doubted that Vera could sway her mother. After all, Vera was the owner of a brothel. Yes, she was Chinese, but did that really mean she knew anything about the superstitious beliefs her mother held or how to dispel them?

* * * *

He'd snatched a couple of folding chairs off the truck that was parked outside the house and simply marched into the garden without being stopped by anybody. In the tent, he placed the chairs around a table while his eyes took in his surroundings.

Various different workers were busy erecting a podium with a canopy on which undoubtedly the ceremony would take place, while others carried in tables and chairs and set them on the wooden boards that had been placed over the grass in order to form an even floor.

From what he could see, none of the workers were vampires. And if one of the humans realized that he didn't belong there, he could use mind control on him and make sure there would be no trouble.

Looking over his shoulder, he made sure nobody was taking any notice of him, and stalked to the door that led into the back of the house. He entered quickly, finding nobody in the large eat-in kitchen. He pushed the door to the hallway open and spied a human standing watch in front of a door. A tall young man who couldn't be older than twenty-five. He could overpower the human within seconds if he had to.

He'd nudged the door open a little wider when the doorbell chimed.

The human sighed and walked to the entrance door, turning his back to him. It was all the time he needed to exit the kitchen and advance silently into the corridor. Quickly, he dove into another room, which he identified as a laundry room by its smell even before he opened the door, and closed the door but for a sliver, so he could spy into the hallway from his hiding place. He was only a few steps away from the stairs that led to the upper floor. That's where he wanted to go to find Ursula's room and wait for her there. Eventually she would go there. All he had to do was wait.

"Hey Samson, Amaury!" the human greeted the two vampires who now entered the foyer.

He felt like growling but suppressed the urge. The boss of Scanguards and one of his high-level partners showing up here was inconvenient. He didn't need any more vampires on the premises than there already were. It was hard enough to avoid the ones already in the house. He had to be careful not to get too close to any of them or they might be able to smell him and realize he didn't belong here, even if he was hidden somewhere. He hoped that the fact that he was hiding in a laundry room that smelled of bleach and laundry soap helped disguise his scent.

"Hey, Blake!" Samson replied.

"What are you guys doing here? I thought you were babysitting Isabelle."

"I left her with Zane."

"Well, in that case, wanna help out?"

Amaury laughed. "Not likely. We're just here to pick up Nina and Delilah."

Blake motioned his head to the door he'd been watching earlier. "They're still in there for the fitting. I'm afraid you can't go in there right now."

Just at that moment, the door opened. The scent drifted to him even before he saw her emerge. Ursula came running out of the room and nearly collided with Amaury's massive frame.

"I'm sorry. I didn't see you, Amaury," she apologized hastily, her voice thick with tears.

"Something wrong?" Amaury wrapped his palm around her forearm when she tried to push past him and head for the stairs.

She shook her head and pulled herself free of his grip. "Nothing!" She sniffed.

Blake made a few steps toward her. "Is it your mother again?"

Ursula nodded.

"What's going on?" Samson asked, his eyes darting back and forth between the two humans.

Ursula turned back to them. "She doesn't like Oliver's date of birth!" A sob dislodged from her chest and she whirled around and ran up the stairs.

"Ah, crap!" Blake cursed.

"Shouldn't one of us go after her and calm her down?" Amaury wondered.

In his hiding place, he narrowed his eyes. No, he didn't want anybody to go after her, because she was just where he wanted her. She'd be in her room, alone, crying her eyes out for whatever reason. She wouldn't even hear him open the door and enter. She would be face-down on her bed. He hadn't thought it would be so easy.

Blake shook his head. "Just give her some time alone. Ursula and her mother have had a few blowouts like that. It'll pass."

When both vampires nodded in agreement, relief washed over

him.

Perfect!

Now he only had to wait for those three to leave the hallway and he would be able to walk upstairs and grab her. Only a few more minutes.

"So, where's Oliver?" Samson asked.

"He's out with Wes. Something about the flowers," Blake replied.

Samson and Amaury exchanged a look. "Excellent. Then he won't be able to overhear us."

"About what?" the human asked curiously.

"About the wedding present. We need your assistance." Amaury motioned to another door, the first one next to the entrance. "Let's go into the study."

Blake tossed a look back at the door he'd been guarding. "But I'm supposed to watch that none of the workers goes in there while the girls are still trying on the bridesmaid's dresses."

"It'll only take a couple of minutes," Samson assured him.

Moments later the three disappeared into the study and closed the door behind them.

He grinned. Finally, things were going his way. He looked up and down the corridor, then pushed the door open wide and approached the staircase, walking on tiptoes. Once he set his foot on the first step, he knew he was safe. The plush carpet on the stairs swallowed the sound of his footsteps as he ascended.

On the landing, he turned and inhaled. He could smell the faint scent of the blood whore's special blood. It made his gums itch. His fangs descended in anticipation of the special treat he was about to enjoy.

He walked along the corridor, each step bringing him closer to his goal. He reached the door and put his hand on the doorknob.

"Ursula!" A female voice came from below. At the same time somebody came running up the stairs.

Cursing silently, his head snapped toward the sound as his feet automatically readied themselves for a quick escape. He caught a glimpse of the back of a head and a red dress as a woman came into view. She hadn't seen him yet, but she would in a second or two when she turned on the landing.

One of the bridesmaids.

But not one of the human ones. She was a vampire, as her aura indicated.

Fuming inside, he dove into the nearest room and closed the door silently behind him.

He could still hear her as she approached Ursula's room and knocked. "Ursula, honey, it's Vera. I calmed her down."

Then the door was opened.

His hands balled into fists while he tried to calm himself. There would be other opportunities like this one.

He just had to be patient.

But for tonight, there were entirely too many vampires in the house. He'd have to get out before anybody recognized him and realized what he was up to.

9

"Red?" Oliver stared at Wes in disbelief as the human brought the car to a stop in front of Quinn's house. "You turned the piglets red?"

Wes shrugged. "Well, it was my first try. I just have to work on the spell. I'm sure the second time it'll work like a charm."

Oliver already started shaking his head before Wesley's last sentence was even out. "No!"

"Oh, come on! I just need a few drops. That's all!" Wes begged, casting him a puppy dog look meant to soften him up.

But Oliver didn't cave. "I said no! Clearly, whatever spell you're trying out isn't working. There's no need wasting any more of my precious blood on it." The only person who'd get his blood would be Ursula. It was part of the blood-bonding ritual, and it would make her immortal while she remained human—and fertile. Once they were bonded, she would be able to conceive his child.

"But I really think it's going to work the second time. I just have to get the dosage right."

Oliver sighed. "Wes, I hate to say this, but don't you think that maybe witchcraft isn't exactly your calling?"

Wesley slammed his flat palm against the steering wheel. "I was born a witch! And I'll be damned if I can't get that back!"

"What do you have to prove? Just find something else that you're good at."

"Easy for you to say! Haven is a vampire, and Kimberly is a great actress. And what am I? Am I the only sibling who can't make anything out of himself? Don't you understand? I want to be somebody. I want to do something useful."

Oliver shook his head, though in a way, he understood Wes all too well. "But you are somebody. You're training as a bodyguard with Scanguards. Isn't that something?"

Wes turned his head away and looked out the side window, staring into the dark. "And you know as well as I how I got that position. Because I offered my blood the night you were turned, Samson felt obligated. Do you think he would really have offered me to train as a bodyguard if I hadn't practically blackmailed him?"

"Are you telling me you're having scruples about that?"

Wes shrugged. "I just wonder sometimes about what would become of me if Hav and Scanguards didn't exist. You know." He glanced at Oliver. "I need to have something that's independent of it. Something that's just mine."

Slowly, Oliver nodded. "I get that. I do. But you can't force it." He reached for the door handle and pushed the car door open. "It'll happen. Just be patient."

Then he exited and walked up to the entrance door. When he reached it, he felt a strange tingling sensation creep up his nape and stopped. He inhaled deeply, picking up many unfamiliar as well as familiar scents. Shaking his head to rid himself of the odd sensation, he pulled his key from his pocket and inserted it into the lock. The motion pushed the door inward. It hadn't been locked.

Cautiously, he stepped into the well-lit interior. Voices drifted to him from the open living room door and the kitchen in the back. Maybe one of the workers had left the door open when he'd left. He would have to speak to Quinn about security at the house during the wedding. It was bad enough that so many contractors marched in and out at all hours of the day, but to know that they were careless and left doors open so that anybody could just walk in off the street was inexcusable.

Just because the latest threats of the operators of the blood brothel and their customers, as well as the vampires who had special mind-control skills and had nearly crushed Scanguards a short while ago, were dealt with, didn't mean they had no enemies.

"Hey, Oliver. Glad I'm catching you alone."

He looked up and saw Maya walk through the living room door and approach him.

"Hey, Maya." He pointed to the bag in her hand, a red dress peeking out of it. "I see you guys tried on your bridesmaid's dresses. Nice color. I had no idea they were red."

She smiled. "A Chinese good luck thing, I guess." She tossed a quick glance over her shoulder. "I just thought I'd let you know. I looked in on your future father-in-law. He's doing fine. I did a blood test, and his doctors are correct. It's just a bit of anemia. Nothing to worry about. I've given him some meds to tide him over until he's back home."

"That's a relief. At least that means we don't have to worry Ursula with it. She's stressed out enough." The last couple of days she'd seemed frazzled most of the time. And he didn't like that look on her, the look that said that she wanted all this to be over.

"Uh, about that."

"What?" he asked, instantly worried.

"Ursula and her mother had another blowout tonight."

He shoved a hand through his hair. "About what?"

"Your date of birth."

"What's my birthday got to do with the wedding?"

"Apparently everything. You have two fours in your date of birth."

"So?"

"In Chinese that's bad luck."

"Damn it! Superstitious crap!"

"Well, of course it's superstition, but it's not any different than Westerners finding Friday the thirteenth unlucky. Unfortunately, it's really upset Ursula." Her eyes turned toward the ceiling.

"I'll take care of it. Thanks, Maya." He ran up the stairs, taking two steps at a time. Nobody had the right to upset the woman he loved, not even his soon-to-be mother-in-law. Particularly not over a stupid thing like a birthday.

Without knocking, he entered the guestroom. "Ursula!"

She wasn't alone. Vera had her arms wrapped around her and stroked her hand over her hair. Both looked up when the door fell shut behind him.

"Just in time," Vera said calmly and rose from the bed.

Immediately, Oliver pulled Ursula into his arms and rubbed his hands over her back. "I'm so sorry, baby. I just heard. Tell me, what can I do?" He looked at her tear-stained eyes, and his heart bled for her.

Before Ursula could answer, Vera replied, "I have an idea of how to fix this."

Oliver looked at her. "How? Last time I checked, nobody could change their birthday at will."

"Well, technically your birthday is the day you were turned into a vampire, which I believe was August 8. And that means you have two 8's in your date of birth, and that's very good luck."

"Yes, but you can't exactly tell Ursula's mother that without telling her I'm a vampire."

"Of course not! But I can use mind control to make her think she heard August 8 instead of April 4 when Rose told her your birthday."

Ursula eased out of his embrace and sat back on her heels. "That's not a solution! We can't keep wiping my parents' memories when something happens that they don't like."

"But we did it after you escaped those vampires. We had to."

"Exactly. We had to!" Ursula said firmly. "But this time we don't.

Just because my mother has some crazy-ass idea about numerology doesn't mean that we have to wipe her memory. We have to reason with her."

Oliver rolled his eyes. "Reason with your mother? Aren't you asking a little too much?"

Ursula braced her hands at her hips. "What are you saying?"

"I'm just saying that she's not likely to listen."

"You don't know her like I do!"

Oliver jumped up from the bed. "Well, I'm not the one who's crying and all upset, am I?"

"I can't believe you said that!"

Shell-shocked, Oliver backed away. Were they just having their first fight? They'd never argued before. For several long moments, he simply stared at Ursula, who held his gaze without flinching.

"Well, no wonder I always dreaded family visits," Vera said calmly. "Brings the worst out in people."

Oliver shot Vera a look, then dropped his head. "I'm sorry." He raised his lids to look at Ursula, slowly placing one foot in front of the other to approach her again. "It's just, I hate seeing you unhappy. It hurts me. Here." He placed his fist over his heart. "I can't stand it when I can't help you."

Ursula reached her arms out to him, and he eased into her embrace, pressing his head against her chest and encircling her with his arms.

"I'm sorry too. It's just all so overwhelming. Every day there's something else that goes wrong."

He lifted his head. "Nothing else will go wrong, I promise you. Our wedding day will be the happiest day in our lives."

A smile formed around her lips. "Are you saying that after our wedding day we won't be as happy again?"

He chuckled. "That's not what I meant."

"What did you mean?"

"Want me to show you?"

"Uhm," Vera's voice interrupted.

Darn, he'd forgotten that Vera was still in the room. He grinned at her sheepishly. "Thank you, Vera, for being there when Ursula needed you."

"No problem."

"What shall we do about your mother now?" Oliver asked.

"Nothing," Ursula said. "My mother is getting what she wants with everything else: the wedding dress, the bridesmaids, the wedding date, and the decorations! But I'm not going to compromise on the groom."

Oliver grinned. "That's my girl!"

10

After much crying, Ursula had reached a truce with her mother. As long as everything else at the wedding was arranged so that it compensated for Oliver's *unfortunate* date of birth, as she called it, she would look past it and not mention it again. This meant that her mother would include every good luck charm she knew in the wedding decorations, almost as if she thought she could ward off the bad luck Oliver's date of birth brought.

Ursula had agreed, not wanting to alienate her mother any further. After all, she was her parents' only child, and this would be the only wedding her mother ever got to arrange.

Finally, the day had arrived. In a few hours, she would be married to Oliver. The house was already swarming with catering staff.

Her mother was still not back from the hairdresser, and her father had decided to take a short nap, claiming he hadn't yet adjusted to the time difference between Washington D.C. and San Francisco.

When she heard a soft rap on the door to her room, she instinctively knew who it was. Was she already feeling the special connection that only blood-bonded couples had? She swore she could sense his presence in the house from the moment he'd entered shortly after sunset.

"Come in."

Oliver slid inside, quickly closing the door behind him. "Hey!" He was still wearing jeans and a T-shirt.

"You'd better not get caught in here or my mother will have a fit!"

He chuckled and pulled her into his arms. "You're not wearing your dress yet, so I think it doesn't count."

Smiling, she wrapped her arms around him and pulled his head to her. "Does the bride get a kiss?"

"Since you're asking so nicely," he murmured, sliding his lips over hers and capturing them.

When his tongue slipped between her lips and started to explore her with long and sensual strokes, she sighed contentedly. She'd missed him during this week, even though she'd seen him every day. But there'd never been a moment for them to be alone. Somebody had always been there.

Oliver's hands roamed her body, his fingers caressing her just like his tongue did. Warmth and desire filled her, rushing through her body like a flashflood. Her entire body tingled pleasantly, and the place between her legs hummed, yearning for a touch. His touch. His kiss. She'd never believed that love could be like this: all consuming, passionate, while at the same time comforting and safe. Yet she felt safe, safe with a vampire, the very creature she had once feared. Oliver had made her forget all her fears and shown her that even a vampire could love.

She felt his love now. It burned brightly and steadily. With every touch and every kiss, she felt it. And tonight, after the ceremony, she would feel it in his bite. His loving bite, how lovingly and silently, he would make her his forever. How he would bestow immortality on her without robbing her of her humanity. How he would make himself vulnerable because once they blood-bonded, Oliver could only feed off her. His body would reject all other blood. In fact, it would make him violently ill if he ever drank blood other than hers.

For a vampire to bond himself to a human required ultimate trust. She felt that trust between them.

When he finally severed the kiss, she breathed heavily.

"We've gotta stop, baby, or there won't be a wedding, because I'll tie you to my bed and won't let you go."

She chuckled. "Would that be so bad?"

He shook his head and wagged his finger playfully. "And deprive myself of seeing you walk down the aisle in your beautiful white dress while—"

"White dress?" she interrupted him.

He pulled back a little, his eyebrows snapping together. "Yes, of course."

"Oliver, I won't be wearing a white dress. My dress is red. White is bad luck at a Chinese wedding. Red is good luck."

She watched as Oliver's facial expression changed to one of dismay. "Uh-oh!"

Trepidation rose in her. "What?"

"You said white is bad? How about white flowers? We can have white flowers, right?" he asked, grimacing.

Her stomach plummeted. "White flowers? Oh, please don't tell me you got white flowers for the wedding." She searched his face.

"I didn't know! I swear I had no idea," he insisted.

Ursula covered her face with her hands. "Oh no! This is not happening!" She sniffed, trying to push back the rising tears. "I should never have told you to take care of the flowers! I should have done it myself. Oh my god, my mother is going to be livid!"

"Baby, I'll fix it!"

She lowered her hands. "You can't fix that! You'll never get that many red flowers now! It's only a few hours till the ceremony. If there'll even be a ceremony! Once my mother sees the flowers, she'll insist we call the whole thing off!"

Oliver cupped her shoulders, forcing her to look at him. "I'll fix it. Whatever it takes! But this wedding will happen tonight, one way or another! I'll get rid of the white flowers. I promise you. When you walk into that tent in a few hours, the flowers will be red. Please trust me!"

The look which he gave her was penetrating. For long seconds, she simply stared back at him. What choice did she have? She had to trust him to make this right. Silently she nodded.

He pressed a quick kiss to her lips and left the room.

Oliver raced down the stairs. Shit! He'd screwed up. He couldn't remember if Ursula had ever told him about not getting white flowers, or whether she'd simply assumed he knew. It didn't matter now. There was no need wasting time by blaming somebody. What was done was done. And now he had to undo it. Swiftly, and without her parents, particularly her mother, noticing.

At the foot of the stairs, he nearly collided with Cain, one of his colleagues. The vampire with the permanent stubble looked as if he'd been born in a tuxedo. Before tonight, he'd only ever seen his fellow bodyguard in street clothes and had no idea how well he wore formalwear.

"Cain, hey!" he greeted him.

Cain glanced at him then the stairs and smirked. "Snuck in a visit to the bride?"

Oliver sighed. "Just as well that I did. Has her mother come back from the hairdresser yet?"

"Haven't seen her." He motioned to the guard who stood at the entrance door. "Bob's been here for the last hour, just like you requested. I've got another one of my men at the side entrance. The catering staff will use the side entrance and the guests the main entrance."

Oliver nodded approvingly. "Thanks for taking care of that. It makes me feel better." A glance at the bodyguard whom Cain had called Bob told him that the man was a vampire. He leaned closer to

Cain and dropped his voice to a low whisper. "And the guy at the tradesmen entrance. Is he a vampire too?"

His colleague nodded.

"Good. I need somebody to watch that Ursula's parents don't enter the tent."

"Something wrong?"

"You could say that."

Cain tilted his head toward the door to the living room. "Thomas and Eddie just arrived. Maybe they can watch the entrance to the tent. I would do it myself, but I still have to do a sweep of the perimeter."

"I'll ask them."

Not losing a second, Oliver marched into the living room. Thomas and Eddie stood near the fireplace, talking in low voices, though he could hear what they were saying thanks to his superior vampire hearing. His vampire colleagues were both blond, but they looked very different tonight. They had exchanged their usual leather biker uniform for elegant black tuxedos and looked like eligible bachelors from a TV show. Only, the two weren't single. In fact, they were married—to each other.

"Thomas, Eddie!" Oliver called out to them, interrupting their— very intimate—conversation. The two lovebirds had only gotten together a short while earlier and by the looks of it were still in their honeymoon phase.

"Oliver, the man of the hour," Thomas replied with a smile.

"Is this how you're getting married?" Eddie asked, shaking his head.

"'Course not. But I need your help right now. Can you guard the tent for me?"

Thomas raised his eyebrows. "You think somebody's gonna walk off with it?"

Ignoring his joke, Oliver said, "Just guard the entrance and make sure that neither Ursula's parents nor any of the other humans enter the tent."

"Sure, we can do that. But why don't you want them to enter the tent?"

"Because the flowers are white, and they need to be red. Or it's bad luck."

Eddie shrugged. "Okay, that makes no sense, but if you want us there, we'll do it, right?" He looked at his partner, who nodded.

"Thanks guys!" Relieved, Oliver rushed out of the room and into the kitchen. Several members of the catering staff were feverishly working on preparing food. But the person he was looking for wasn't in the room. Leaving the kitchen, he pulled out his cell and dialed a number.

"Yeah?" Wesley replied.

"I need you to do me a favor. Can you come to the house right now?" Oliver walked along the corridor when the door to the basement and garage opened.

"I'm already here." Wes stepped through the door. Behind him, Haven appeared, and a moment later, Blake.

"You're not dressed yet?" Blake asked. "The guests will start arriving soon."

"What were you guys doing down there?" Oliver asked, ignoring Blake's question. It would take him all of five minutes to get dressed.

Wes gave a noncommittal grunt and brushed some dust from the sleeve of his tuxedo. "Nothing. What's up?"

"There's a problem with the flowers."

"What problem?" Wes asked. "They looked perfect when they came this morning. I made sure of it. Hey, if they screwed something up after that, it's not my fault! Besides, I was doing you a favor!"

Oliver grabbed his friend by the shoulder. "Hey! I'm not blaming you. It's not your fault. It's mine. They're the wrong color. We can't have white flowers at the wedding. It's bad luck. I need them to be red."

Wes tossed him a not-my-problem-look. "There's no way you can get a florist to supply that many red flower arrangements in the short time we've got left. Even if you went to several florists, they wouldn't have enough to replace all the current ones."

"For once, Wes is right," Haven added.

Wes glared at his brother. "I said I'm sorry! Okay? I'll deal with the dogs after the wedding."

"You mean the pigs?" Blake threw in, chuckling.

Wes whirled around to Blake. "You're not helping!"

"Stop it!" Oliver ground out. "That's not important now. What's important is that Wesley turned the pigs red." And that unfortunate incident would now provide the solution to his problem.

Haven loosened his bow tie. "Well, at least somebody agrees that my little brother has no business practicing witchcraft." He tossed a sideways glance at Wes.

"One of these days you're going to change your opinion on that," Wes warned.

"Quiet!" Oliver shouted, and at last all three fell silent and stared at him as if he'd finally lost it. Maybe he had. "Wes, I need your help. You have to turn the flowers in the tent red. Now. Before Ursula's parents see them."

"How?"

"You turned the pigs red. Use the same spell!"

A wide grin spread over Wesley's face. "Does that mean you're going to donate a little more of your blood?"

"Just for this one spell," Oliver conceded.

Wesley dug into his inside pocket and pulled out a glass vial.

"You always carry a vial around with you?" Blake asked.

Wesley winked at him. "First rule of a bodyguard: you've always gotta be prepared."

Haven rolled his eyes. "More like first rule of an opportunist."

Wes shrugged. "I need a few things from your pantry too. And a few minutes to mix the potion. Preferably where nobody can walk in on us."

"The gym downstairs," Oliver suggested.

Instantly, all three shook their heads.

"How about in the laundry room?" Haven suggested instead.

"That'll work."

It took fifteen minutes after Oliver had *donated* some blood before Wesley's potion was ready for use. Making sure Thomas and Eddie were at their places to watch that nobody entered the tent, Haven stood inside the tent, blocking the walkway to the tradesmen entrance so none of the catering staff would disturb them during the spell, while Blake blocked the kitchen door so none of the waiters or kitchen staff could look into the tent from there.

"Do your thing," Oliver said, waving his arms at the white flower arrangements that stood on the tables and decorated the podium as well as the rods that held the tent up.

There were tables and chairs for over a hundred guests in the tent. While the tablecloths were white, the white covers for the chairs sported red bows. And the napkins were equally red. He had to admit he liked the rich color. It reminded him of Ursula's blood.

"Step back," Wesley warned and walked into the middle of the tent.

Oliver heard him mumble something incoherent—presumably the spell—before he tossed the vial with the potion on the ground.

Instinctively Oliver took another step back when red smoke rose from the broken glass vial. As it swirled around, one by one the flowers turned red. But the flowers weren't the only things that took on the magical color: the tablecloths and chair covers also turned red.

Oliver shrugged. It couldn't hurt.

Wesley turned around to him, smiling broadly.

Next to Oliver, Haven hissed in a breath. Then he took a few steps toward his brother, hugged him roughly, and slapped him on the shoulder. "You did well, Wes! I'm proud of you."

If Oliver didn't have enhanced vampire vision, he would have missed the wet sheen that built in Wesley's eyes as a reaction to his big brother's compliment.

Finally Wesley had achieved something to win the approval of his brother. Maybe screwing up on the flowers hadn't been so bad after all.

Oliver smiled. Nothing else could go wrong now.

11

For almost two hours he'd watched all the guests arrive. Nobody noticed him standing in the shadow of a hedge on the other side of the street. They were too busy parading in their fancy clothes. More humans than vampires arrived for the event, many of the humans Chinese. Clearly, the bride had a large extended family, though none of her relatives seemed to carry the special blood. Even from across the street he would have been able to smell it, so attuned was he to it.

Human valets were parking the guests' cars, and a vampire guard at the entrance door checked the invitations. Another vampire guard stood at the tradesmen entrance through which the service personnel, the waiters and kitchen staff, entered.

He'd dressed appropriately. In his black tuxedo he would blend in with the guests as if he belonged there. Only the vampires on the premises would know he didn't. But soon they would all be in the tent at the back of the house, and the only one he'd have to deal with was the one guarding the entrance door.

The house was lit like a Christmas tree. It made it easy for him to watch the goings-on. When the living room started to empty out, he knew that the guests were taking their places in the tent. It couldn't be much longer now.

He lifted his eyes to the upper floor. In one of the rooms, Ursula would be waiting, alone, while everybody else would be in the tent.

It was time.

Calmly, he crossed the street and walked up to the entrance door, out of sight of the vampire guarding the side entrance. The door to the house was open, but blocking it was a vampire guard. The guy didn't know him, and that was his advantage.

He flashed a charming smile at the guard. "I hope I'm not late."

The vampire motioned to the interior. "It's going to start in a few minutes." Then he nodded to him. "Your name? And your invitation please."

"Michael Valentine," he answered and reached into his jacket pocket. "Uh, and here's my invitation."

With a single swift move, he pulled a stake from his inside pocket and plunged it into the guard's heart, before the man could even react.

The vampire disintegrated into dust. Michael turned to assure himself that the vampire guarding the side door hadn't heard anything suspicious. There was no sound coming from the tradesmen entrance. Quickly he swept the set of keys, cell phone, and loose change that remained from the vampire into the bushes.

Unimpeded, he entered the house. Without hesitation, he walked up the stairs, when he heard the music in the tent starting. But there would be no ceremony. No wedding. No blood-bond.

I'm coming for you, Ursula.

* * * *

"I think that's our cue," her father said when music came drifting up from the tent.

Ursula turned away from the full-length mirror in the guestroom and faced him.

He smiled back at her. "You look beautiful, Wei Ling. You're a woman now. You make us very proud, me and your mother."

"Even though I'm not marrying a Chinese man?"

"That was never very important to me." He chuckled. "Now, your mother, that's another story. But she'll get used to it. Don't worry about it."

"Thank you, Dad." She leaned toward him and kissed him on the cheek.

For a moment, she hesitated. There was so much she wanted to tell him, to confess who Oliver was and what he'd done for her. How he'd rescued her from a life in shackles. Her parents knew nothing of it. After her release from the blood brothel, Oliver and Scanguards had gone through great lengths to wipe her parents' memories and done the same with everybody who knew about her three-year disappearance. But there were moments like these when she wanted to tell the truth, though she knew it would only lead to pain.

"I love you, Dad," she whispered instead. "For everything you and Mom have done for me."

Somewhat embarrassed, her father smiled. "Time to go and meet your husband."

"I don't think so!" A menacing male voice came from the door as it shut behind him.

Ursula whirled her head around to the intruder and almost tripped over her long red dress. Her breath caught in her throat when she recognized the man. Though she didn't remember his name, she knew he was one of the former clients of the blood brothel. Leeches, she and the other girls had called them.

"What is this?" her father asked, outraged. "Get out!"

"Only once I have what I want!" the vampire snarled, his eyes now glaring red, and his fangs descending.

Her father gasped, but Ursula knew the vampire's look all too well. He'd come for her blood.

"What are you?!" her father choked out as he moved in front of Ursula as if to protect her.

But Ursula knew her father was no match for the vampire. No

human was. She squeezed past him, glaring at the leech.

"Oliver will kill you if you harm me!" she warned.

"He won't catch us. We'll be long gone by the time he realizes."

At his words, Ursula shook her head in disbelief. No! He hadn't simply come to attack her here and drink her blood, he was planning to kidnap her!

"No!" she screamed, but she knew that the music in the tent would prevent her scream from reaching Oliver's ears. He would stand there at the podium, waiting for her in vain. Waiting, while she was being kidnapped.

"Now come to me, and I won't hurt you," the vampire promised, then added, " . . . much."

"Leave my daughter alone, you monster!" her father yelled and jumped toward him before she could stop him.

"No! Dad! No!"

But it was too late. With one punch, the vampire knocked her father clear across the room and into the wall, where he collapsed with a groan.

"Oh no! Dad! No!" She ran her eyes over his body. She couldn't see any blood, but the impact could have left internal injuries. Inside her, anger and worry collided. "You'll pay for this!"

The vampire chuckled, and the sound made her shiver in disgust. Like a tiger, he approached, setting one foot in front of the other. Slowly, as if he enjoyed this and didn't want it to end too soon. Like a cat playing with a mouse.

Frantically she looked around the room for anything she could use as a weapon, but came up empty.

She was at his mercy now.

"I've waited for this for so long," her attacker confessed. "All those days in my cold cell I was dreaming of this, of finding another blood whore. I'd almost given up."

"Get away from me!" she warned again. "Oliver will kill you."

A moan from where her father had collapsed told her he was alive. She cast a quick glance in his direction and realized he was trying to move, but struggled.

"Maybe," the vampire hedged. "But only after I've gotten what I wanted." He fletched his fangs and took another step toward her.

Like a cold fist, fear clamped around her heart. She could see it in his eyes now: the madness. He wouldn't be able to stop drinking from her once he started. He would drain her.

Tonight, on her wedding night, she would die. And her father would have to watch helplessly.

12

Oliver watched as Blake tied the wedding rings onto the tiny pink pillow and handed it to Isabelle. The toddler grinned up at them, looking adorable in her pink dress. Together with Delilah, they all stood at the French doors of the living room that led to the tented walkway leading into the tent. The music from the tent where a string quartet played came through the loudspeakers into the living room.

"You sure she's gonna be able to do that?" Oliver asked and grinned.

Delilah exchanged a look with her daughter. "Of course she is. Aren't you, Isabelle?"

The toddler beamed.

"Now go into the tent just like we practiced."

Isabelle turned around and staggered along the path, still a little wobbly on her feet. Delilah followed her closely, ready to catch her if she fell.

"Well, it's almost time," Blake said, grinning. "You can still change your mind, you know. I'll take her off your hands in a heartbeat."

Oliver boxed him in the side. "Not a chance."

His half-brother chuckled. "Just thought I'd give it one last shot."

"Hey, thanks for being my best man."

"Glad you asked me."

Suddenly the door to the corridor opened. "Are we too late?" a familiar voice asked.

Oliver swiveled on his heels and saw Dr. Drake rushing in, his Barbie-doll receptionist on his arm.

"Sorry, I hope this is the right entrance, but there was nobody telling us which way to go. Luckily the door was open." He shrugged apologetically.

"The guard outside should have directed you," Oliver said.

"What guard?"

Oliver's heart stopped. Without answering, he charged past Drake and rushed into the foyer. He ripped the entrance door open, but the vampire guard Cain had stationed there was gone. He turned back toward the foyer when he stepped on something. He bent down and inspected the item. A dime was wedged between the grout of two travertine tiles.

Though finding a lost coin wasn't something unusual, the hairs on Oliver's nape rose and a cold shiver ran down his spine.

Something wasn't right. Cain would have never pulled the guard off his post.

Blake came running from the living room. "What's going on?"

Oliver was already charging toward the stairs leading to the upper floors. "Alert Cain and have him sweep the premises for any intruders. Discreetly. I don't want anybody to alarm the guests."

"Got it."

But Oliver barely heard Blake's reply. He'd been a bodyguard long enough to know when to listen to his gut feeling. And his gut feeling told him to make sure Ursula was safe. That it was presumably bad luck to see the bride in her wedding dress before the wedding didn't matter.

When he entered the upper floor, his suspicion was confirmed. Ursula was in danger. A muffled cry drifted to his sensitive ears. A human wouldn't have heard it, but he had.

He flung the door to the guestroom open and barreled into the room, assessing the situation within a split second without slowing his movements.

A vampire pressed Ursula against the wall, his hands preventing her from fighting against him, though she kicked her legs against his shins, while the vampire's head neared her neck. Panic and desperation shone from Ursula's eyes. A few yards away, Yao Bang struggled to rise from the floor but appeared weak and dazed.

The vampire's head whirled around, noticing Oliver instantly. He snarled, his eyes glaring red, his fangs protruding from his lips. Oliver recognized him now. He was one of the addicts that Scanguards had treated.

"Michael Valentine!" Oliver ground out.

Valentine narrowed his eyes and moved so fast a human would only see a blur, bringing Ursula in front of his body like a shield, his arm wrapping around her upper arms so she couldn't move them, and the claws of his other hand pressing against the soft flesh of her throat.

"One move and I'll slice her open!" he warned.

Oliver arrested in his movement. He couldn't risk Ursula's life, and he knew that one slice of Valentine's sharp claws across her neck would kill her almost instantly. Oliver wouldn't even have enough time to turn her into a vampire to save her life. She would die.

He had to buy himself some time. "You won't kill her," Oliver hedged. "You want her special blood."

A flicker in Valentine's eyes confirmed that he'd guessed right. The vampire was still an addict. Zane had been right. Rehab hadn't worked on everybody.

"Get away from the door!" Valentine ordered.

"No!"

Oliver flicked his gaze to Ursula, who had been the one to voice the protest.

"Don't do it. Don't let him take me. I'd rather die than be

imprisoned again." Her eyes pleaded with him.

He knew what was going through her mind. If Valentine took her, she would face the same ordeal as she had for three years while imprisoned in the blood brothel.

"I won't let him take you," he promised her.

"I don't see how you can prevent it," Valentine said and started walking sideways, pulling Ursula with him.

"The house is crawling with vampires. You'll never get out!"

From where Ursula's father lay on the floor, a gasp came. But Oliver couldn't turn his face to look at Yao Bang, though he knew his eyes were open and he was watching them in horror.

Valentine let out a mocking laugh. "They're all in the tent in the back of the house." He motioned to the window. "We're going out the front."

Oliver was poised, readying himself to attack. His eyes searched the room for any weapon because he carried none in his elegant tuxedo. There had been no place to conceal a stake.

A few more steps and Valentine would be at the window. Oliver's breathing accelerated. He had to do something now.

As Valentine dragged Ursula with him, her dress caught in the legs of a chair and she stumbled sideways. Valentine held on to her, but the claws on her throat slipped momentarily.

Seeing his chance, Oliver pounced. His claws lengthened in mid-flight, and his arm pulled back for leverage then swung forward to punch Valentine's shoulder to knock him back and make him lose his grip on Ursula.

Ursula fell, her balance uprooted by the power of the impact. Her legs, already tangled in her long dress and the petticoats beneath, lost their footing, and she fell forward. From the corner of his eye, Oliver saw her reach for the chair to brace her fall, but he couldn't help her, because Valentine's claws were coming toward him in a one-two punch that knocked Oliver's head sideways.

Without as much as a breath in between, Oliver aimed a fist at Valentine and hit the side of his neck, whipping him sideways. As Valentine fell against the window frame, Oliver's eyes darted around. But there was no time to find anything to fashion a stake from.

Valentine pushed himself off the window frame with such speed and agility that Oliver was taken by surprise when his attacker body-slammed him, tackling him to the ground. Oliver landed hard with his back on the wooden floor, making the floorboards moan in protest.

A claw came toward him, but Oliver blocked it with his forearm, pushing back while he twisted underneath his attacker. The rage flowing through his veins gave him added strength, and he managed to toss Valentine off him. However, his opponent was agile and found his feet at the same time as Oliver rose to his own.

This time, Oliver didn't let Valentine's next punch find its intended target. Instead, Oliver twisted on his heels and evaded him gracefully.

Their combined grunts and groans filled the room and mingled with the heavy breathing of Yao Bang and Ursula, who'd both managed to get to their feet.

Ursula had run to her father, and from the corner of his eye, Oliver caught a glimpse of the two as Ursula tried to calm her father, while her eyes darted around the room, seemingly looking for something. But he couldn't concentrate on her, because fending off Valentine's kicks and punches took all his concentration. And in the uncomfortable tuxedo, he felt less mobile than usual, though his opponent had the same handicap, wearing a tuxedo as well.

With every blow, Oliver realized more and more that he and his opponent were of equal strength. They were equally tall and well built. What he needed was an advantage. Because it could be minutes until one of his colleagues came up to this floor to find them.

Oliver gritted his teeth and punched harder. Valentine swayed on his feet, giving Oliver hope that he was tiring, but it wasn't the case, as he found out an instant later. As fast as a bullet train, the other vampire jumped to the side, gripped the chair, and slammed it against the wall, breaking it.

"Shit!" Oliver cursed, as he saw Valentine clamp his hand around one of the wooden legs that had broken off.

Now his opponent had a stake.

The evil grin on Valentine's face confirmed that the bastard couldn't wait to use it.

"Guess that's it," Valentine said with a self-congratulatory smirk, then jumped toward Oliver.

The power of the impact slammed Oliver backward and the back of his knees hit the bed frame, making him tumble onto the bed, landing in a supine position. Valentine jumped onto him, pinning him and trapping one of his arms under his knee.

With his free arm, Oliver fought his attacker as best he could, but Valentine had both arms available to fight. On his left Oliver perceived a movement, something red clouding his vision, but he didn't dare turn his eyes away from Valentine.

Triumphantly, the other vampire lifted the stake while Oliver tried to push him back with his free arm. To no avail: the hand holding the stake lowered.

"Fuck!" he pressed out from between clenched teeth.

Oliver heard a cracking sound. Had a bone in his forearm broken? He couldn't tell for sure, but he only knew that he couldn't hold Valentine off much longer. And once Valentine had killed him, there was nobody stopping him from getting Ursula.

"No!" he screamed. "Noooooo!"

With his last ounce of strength, he pushed Valentine back, managing to catapult him off him. Valentine staggered backward a few paces, when he suddenly stopped dead in his tracks, his eyes widening in surprise and shock.

A groan came from his throat. Then he disintegrated into dust.

Behind him, Ursula stood, her arm stretched out, holding a makeshift stake. He recognized it as a piece of the chair. It hadn't been his forearm breaking. Ursula had broken a leg off the chair and used it as a stake.

She had saved him.

Oliver jumped from the bed and ran toward her, wordlessly pulling her into his arms. He pressed her trembling body to him. For a few moments, he couldn't speak.

"It's over," she murmured.

"I'm so sorry." He kissed her.

From the hallway, several people came running. Cain burst into the room first, followed by Blake and Zane.

"Where is he?" Cain yelled.

Oliver pointed to the floor where dust had settled. "He's dead."

Cain sighed in relief. "He killed Bob, who was stationed at the front door. I found some of his belongings. Who was he?"

"Michael Valentine."

"Fuck!" Zane cursed. He'd been the one who'd first interrogated Michael Valentine when he'd come to Scanguards' attention. And Zane had also been the one who had guessed that rehab wouldn't work on all the addicted vampires.

"You were right. Rehab didn't work for all of them," Oliver said to Zane. Then his gaze fell on Yao Bang who still stood where Ursula had left him only moments earlier, looking at them cautiously. He appeared uninjured.

"Buy us some time downstairs," Oliver ordered, looking at Blake.

"And say what?"

"Wardrobe malfunction. Whatever," Oliver said. Then he looked at Zane and Cain. "Are we sure he was the only one?"

Both nodded. "Positive."

"Good. Then give us some privacy." He motioned to Yao Bang and his colleagues nodded knowingly. They realized what he had to do now.

When the door closed behind the two vampires, Oliver looked at Ursula. She ran to her father and wrapped her arms around him. "Are you hurt?"

He shook his head. "Just a few bruises."

"We have to wipe his memory," Oliver said to her, avoiding her father's eyes.

Ursula nodded with a grim expression on her face. "I'm sorry, Dad, but it's for the better. You should have never seen this."

Oliver took a step toward him, but Yao Bang stretched out his hand as if to stop him. "Please don't!"

"It won't hurt. I promise you. You won't even know."

Yao Bang shook his head. "Please. Whatever you're gonna do, don't do it. Leave me my memories." He pointed to the floor where the vampire had died. "I don't *want* to forget what dangers are out there."

Ursula shook her head vehemently. "Dad! Please! You'll only worry if you know."

Yao Bang's eyes softened when he looked at his daughter. "Wei Ling, my little one, but I've worried until now. I've always worried about your safety. When you moved to New York to go to university, I worried about you. Because there is so much evil in the world. Now I won't have to worry any longer. Don't you see?" He pointed to Oliver. "Now I know you'll be protected."

Oliver watched as Ursula's forehead wrinkled in surprise. "But aren't you shocked that I'm going to marry a vampire?"

A kind smile curved her father's lips upward. "He loves you. When he attacked the other vampire to save you, he didn't hesitate even a split second." Then he shrugged. "Though I guess a vampire wouldn't have been my first choice, particularly since I didn't think they existed. But at least that means he can protect you from other vampires."

Ursula sighed.

"Please, by leaving me my memories, you're granting me peace of mind," Yao Bang pleaded.

Oliver exchanged a look with Ursula, then he took a step toward her father and stretched out his hand. "I have your word that you'll never divulge our secret?"

Yao Bang nodded and took Oliver's hand. "I promise you, son."

It was the first time his future father-in-law had ever called him son.

"What about my mother?" Ursula interrupted.

"Let me handle your mother," Ursula's father promised. "I'll find a way to tell her if it ever becomes necessary." Then he brushed some dirt particles off his tuxedo. "And now, I think it's time to get on with this wedding or your mother is going to have a fit."

Oliver chuckled. "I'd better get cleaned up a little."

Ursula giggled. "I've got *vampire* all over my dress." She pointed to the dust on her skirt.

Their gazes met and heated in an instant. In a few short hours she would have *vampire* all over her body. Her naked body.

13

From his vantage point on the small podium in the tent, Oliver looked down the aisle. He couldn't see Ursula, but he knew she was standing at the French doors to the living room, ready to walk along the covered walkway into the tent. He'd made sure that nothing else would happen now. Zane and Cain had volunteered to remain in the living room with her and her father until they were safely inside the tent. And once they were married, Oliver would blood-bond her as soon as possible. Only then would she truly be safe. Because only then would they be able to communicate telepathically with each other. And Oliver would always immediately sense when she was in danger.

He tried to relax and watched as Isabelle walked down the middle of the aisle, carrying the little pillow with the rings in her hands. Delilah coached her from the sidelines, making sure she didn't stop midway, but walked all the way to the front.

When he got his first glimpse of Ursula walking on her father's arm, coming closer with each step, he held his breath. During the fight and the few moments afterwards, he hadn't had a chance to admire her and take in how truly beautiful she looked. He'd never thought that she could look more glorious in a red wedding dress than any other woman in a white one. As graceful as a princess, she walked toward him, her eyes focused on him. All fear and panic was wiped from her face.

His heart started to thunder and he feared that everybody in the tent could hear how wildly it beat. Because it beat for her. And because of her.

When Ursula and her father finally stopped at the podium, he exchanged a brief look with Yao Bang. A contented smile played around the older man's lips. Even though Oliver didn't know his father-in-law very well, he grew fonder of him by the minute. To be accepted by Ursula's father so wholeheartedly warmed his heart. His gaze drifted over the guests. Quinn sat near the podium. His sire looked at him as proudly as any father would, and behind him, Samson beamed with a happy smile. He'd been the first to see potential in him and had offered him a chance for a new life. Without Samson and Quinn he wouldn't be here today.

He tore his look from them and smiled at Ursula. Their gazes fused.

Oliver barely heard the words of the minister as he spoke an introductory prayer and Yao Bang answered him when asked who was giving this woman to this man. Then he took his seat next to his wife.

Seconds turned into minutes as they exchanged traditional vows. The only thing they had changed was the ending. They'd replaced "till death do us part" with more suitable words.

" . . . for eternity," Oliver now said and felt tears rise into his eyes when he saw the wet sheen covering Ursula's irises.

"The rings," the minister prompted and looked at Blake.

His best man crouched down to Isabelle and nodded at her, giving her a sign that it was her turn, and the toddler staggered toward the minister, holding the pillow with the rings in front of her. She glanced sideways as if to seek approval from her mother, when she tripped and fell forward. But the little hybrid's reflexes were as sharp as those of a vampire, and she braced her fall with her hands before her knees could hit the floorboards, though she dropped the pillow in the process.

A collective gasp raced through the guests, but Isabelle lifted her head with a wide smile, looking almost apologetic. Two tiny fangs flashed from her open mouth.

Oliver had never seen anything more adorable. He and Ursula had never spoken about children, but he knew that eventually they would have some. Once they were both ready.

It appeared the minister had seen Isabelle's fangs, because his forehead pulled together and he leaned toward the toddler.

"Isabelle!" Blake chastised under his breath, and she seemed to understand him and quickly pressed her lips together again. She reached for the pillow that had fallen from her hands, and with Blake's help, she was back on her feet within seconds. "That a girl," Blake praised, winking at Oliver.

Oliver suppressed a chuckle.

The minister took the rings and blessed them before handing one to Ursula and one to him.

When Ursula repeated the minister's words, Oliver's heart expanded, filling with love and pride, with joy and happiness.

"With this ring, I thee wed." Ursula slid the ring onto his finger.

Oliver didn't wait for the minister to prompt him, impatient for Ursula to be his wife. "With this ring, I thee wed."

Nor did he wait for the minister to tell him that he could kiss the bride. He simply pulled Ursula into his arms and kissed her.

"I now pronounce you man and wife." He heard the minister's words somewhere in the distance.

"I love you," he whispered against his bride's lips only for her to hear, though he knew that the vampires in the tent would be able to pick up his words. And maybe even the humans, for it was a feeling he couldn't hide from anybody. Nor did he intend to.

14

They had danced. They had cut the cake. They had toasted to their guests, listened to speeches, and accepted well-wishes, while secretly wishing they could escape and be alone.

Somebody finally had mercy on them and announced that it was time the bride and groom withdrew, while the rest of the guests could continue to celebrate. That somebody was Quinn.

Holding Ursula's hand, Oliver now walked to the door of the gym which was located in the basement in one corner of the large garage, still thinking about Quinn's words that their wedding present would be down there and the subsequent sparkle in Rose's eyes. As if they had set up a prank.

He knew all about wedding pranks: toilet-paper-wrapped furniture, shaving-cream-decorated cars, confetti-littered beds, the things that your best friends did to the apartment while the couple was still dancing at the wedding reception. Oliver couldn't care less what prank they'd set up, because nothing could erase the relief he felt knowing Ursula was safe now. He'd almost lost her tonight, and he needed to wipe out those memories by making new ones with her.

Oliver turned the doorknob and pushed the door inward. Then he froze, not in shock, but in wonder.

Next to him, Ursula sucked in a breath. "Oh my god!"

The gym equipment was gone.

"It's beautiful," she whispered.

He could only echo her words. This was the best wedding gift Quinn and Rose could have ever given them: a place to consummate their blood-bond away from any curious eyes and ears. A place just for them.

In the center of the small room stood a large bed draped with soft sheets, a canopy of sheer material over it. The fabric that flowed all the way to the floor, covered with plush rugs, turned the bed into a cocoon. Along the walls, sconces with candles had been installed, and the subdued light made the room glow as if a fireplace were burning. It looked like a dream.

Oliver tore his gaze from the bed and looked at his wife. The word still felt so new, but it felt right.

"There were moments when I thought this would never happen," he said, his hand reaching up to stroke his knuckles over the elegant curve of Ursula's neck.

"I was scared," she confessed.

"I'll make sure you'll never be scared again." He leaned in to brush his lips over her cheek.

Ursula's arms slid around his neck, pulling him against her body. "I missed you."

"Not as much as I missed you." The last few days had been hell. Finally they were past them. "This week I thought I would have to break into my own house just so I could feel you in my arms."

She laughed softly. "Break in? Maybe I would have opened the door for you."

"Maybe?" he growled, dropping his lips to her neck and nibbling there.

"If you'd asked nicely."

He loved it how Ursula teased him, how she seduced him with her sinful voice while she rubbed her tantalizing body against his. "How nicely?" He pressed his hard-on against her soft stomach, letting her feel what she did to him.

"Oh," she murmured. "As nicely as you're asking now." Her hand slid to his backside, squeezing him through his tuxedo.

Oliver lifted his head. "I'm glad we're speaking the same language."

"I am too. But were you planning on talking all night, or would you rather we do something else?" She tilted her head toward the bed.

"Well, since you're asking so nicely . . . "

Oliver slid his mouth over hers and kissed her. He stroked his tongue over the seam of her lips and felt them part under light pressure. Without haste, he drove his tongue into her mouth and explored her. No matter how often he'd kissed her in the last few months, it was different now. Tonight she had become his wife, and in a few moments she would become his blood-bonded mate. This kiss was the kiss that would start the rest of their lives. He had no intention of rushing this.

This would be the memory they'd always cherish, the one that would help them overcome any obstacle in the future, any quarrels they might find themselves in, any disagreements or misunderstandings that might arise between them. It would make them stronger as a couple. Their union would be unbreakable. And last longer than one lifetime. Their love would last an eternity.

"I love you," Oliver murmured, briefly breaking the kiss before capturing her mouth again and pouring every ounce of passion and love he felt for Ursula into the kiss.

They undressed each other slowly. Layer by layer of clothing fell to the floor, first his tuxedo jacket and shirt, then her wedding dress. Finally his pants, until they stood in front of each other only in their underwear.

Ursula's strapless bra and panties were as red as her dress, but there was a different color he noticed. He slid his finger under the blue garter she wore around one of her thighs.

"Something blue," he whispered, smiling. "I wanted to incorporate some Western traditions too. You were so accommodating in accepting everything Asian my parents threw at you. I wanted to thank you."

Oliver licked his lips. "I like the way you think."

She pointed to her ankle, making him look down. "Something borrowed."

Oliver spotted the diamond ankle bracelet she wore. "Whose?"

"Nina lent it to me."

"I like it. I think I should buy you one of your own."

She smiled. "I think you should."

"How about something old?" he asked.

Ursula reached to the back of her head and took out the sparkling comb that held up her hair. The red comb was decorated with gold Chinese symbols. "It was my grandmother's. My mother wore it for her wedding."

"It's beautiful." Then he looked into her eyes. "But nothing can ever be as beautiful as you." He kissed her, pulling her against the curve of his body, feeling her soft skin against his. Instantly, his entire body was in flames.

"Don't you want to know what's new?" Ursula asked, pulling back slightly.

"Later." Impatiently he tore at her bra, unhooking it and sliding it off her.

He put his palms over her small but firm breasts, squeezing them. Ursula moaned softly.

Gently, he urged her to take a few steps back, directing her toward the bed. When the back of her legs hit the mattress, he lowered her onto it. She looked perfect on the white sheets, like a present he didn't deserve. His eyes ran over her body, drinking her in.

He braced himself on the bed with one knee and one hand, hovering over her, while his other hand caressed her silken skin, reacquainting himself with her body. A week of not touching her had been too long.

His fingers trailed down the valley between her breasts and crossed her flat stomach until they reached the red silk of her panties. He slid underneath it, combing through her thatch of hair, and felt her spread her legs wider.

The scent of her arousal wafted to him, and he soaked it in, allowing it to drug him. Then his finger slipped lower and touched her moist cleft.

A hitched breath came from Ursula, then another one as he traveled along her slit and bathed his fingers in her wetness. Her flesh quivered. He loved how receptive she was whenever he touched her. And he loved arousing her. And making her surrender in his arms. Just as he was going to do now. With his hands and his mouth.

Oliver used both his hands to pull her panties down and free her from them, but when he looked at her naked body, he noticed something different. He lifted his head to stare at her. She met his gaze.

"Something new," she whispered.

He dropped his gaze back to the small tattoo that sat just above the left edge of her pubic hair: a Chinese symbol and within it, the initials U and O were intertwined.

"It means forever," she said.

"I love it."

He lowered his lips onto the tattoo and kissed it. Then he shifted on the bed and took his place between her spread legs, bringing his mouth to her weeping pussy. His tongue swiped along her moist folds, gathering the wetness that coated them, tasting her sweet essence. Her soft moans and sighs provided the background music to his caresses, and her hands drove into his hair, making him shiver with pleasure. As she spread her thighs wider, offering herself to him, he slid his hands under her backside and tilted her sex, giving him better access. His tongue drove into her inviting slit, then moved higher to brush over the tiny organ at the base of her curls.

Ursula writhed underneath him, and he tightened his hold on her,

shifting his hands to the front of her thighs to hold her down as he licked and sucked her with more intensity. He tried to ignore his aching cock that was still confined within his boxer briefs. He knew he couldn't yet free himself of the last piece of clothing, or he would attack her like the hungry beast he was. Because tasting Ursula and making love to her brought out everything primal in him. Civility was pushed into the background, humanity obliterated. All that was left inside him was pure vampire: ravenous, insatiable, intense.

The urge to make her his was stronger now. The vampire inside him knew that this was the night of their blood-bond, that tonight they would become one. And the vampire was impatient.

His hips jerked against the mattress, moving back and forth to grant his cock some measure of relief. To no avail. Oliver knew that there was only one way he could get relief: inside of Ursula's body.

Growling, he licked her clit faster and harder. Ursula thrashed, her body so close to release he could almost taste it. Sweat dripped from his face and neck, and to his horror he could feel his hands turn into claws, his fingernails sharpen to spiky barbs.

"Oh God!" Ursula called out.

Then a shudder raced through her body, visibly shaking her as her orgasm claimed her.

The vampire inside him broke to the surface, unleashed by the call from his mate. His claws sliced through his boxer briefs, freeing him at last. Cool air blasted against his burning cock, but only for a second. Faster than ever before, he thrust into her, seating himself to the hilt. A choked breath escaped her throat as her interior muscles imprisoned him, still quivering from her orgasm.

Unable to hold himself back, Oliver pulled halfway out of her tight sheath then plunged back inside. And again. His vampire side went wild, fucking her hard and fast.

"I'm sorry!" he cried out. "I don't want to hurt you!"

He'd always thought the bonding would be a tender affair, a slow merging of bodies, a gentle lovemaking. He hadn't counted on his vampire side taking over so completely and giving him no choice in the matter.

He watched as his claw sliced into his own shoulder to create a small bleeding wound, before he lowered it to her face.

"Drink from me!" he demanded, his voice gruff and barely recognizable.

Ursula should reject him, afraid of what he would do to her, yet she did nothing of the sort. Instead, she placed her lips over the incision and licked it, lapping up the blood that oozed from it.

His entire body shuddered.

"Oh God!" he murmured.

He'd never felt anything like it. It was like the most sensual caress. The most tender embrace. The movements of his body slowed, becoming more gentle and tender. Then his eyes zoomed in on the throbbing vein at her neck, how it beckoned to him, called to him to take her.

In slow motion, he lowered his lips to it, feeling her shiver when he connected with her skin. Without haste, he opened his mouth and grazed her with the tips of his fangs. Slowly, they pierced her skin, descending into her flesh.

He drew on her vein. Blood rushed into his mouth and cascaded down his throat. He'd drunk from her many times before, but his time was different. This time she drank from him too. It created a circle, an unbreakable bond between them.

Ursula's hand slid to his nape and pressed him to her.

Take me, all of me, he heard her thoughts drift to him and knew their bond had been established.

The knowledge that they were one now catapulted him over the edge. His climax blasted through his body like a tsunami, unstoppable and uncontrollable.

Ursula's muscles spasmed and he could now feel her orgasm as it traveled through her in waves, just like she would be able to sense his climax and experience it as if she were inhabiting his body.

So beautiful, he thought.

Will it always be this way? she asked, continuing to drink his blood, just as he still sucked at her vein.

Yes, always.

Because he would make sure that they would always be as happy as they were now. Whatever it took. Because she was his life, just as he was hers.

THE END

Sign up for the 1001 Dark Nights Newsletter
and be entered to win a Tiffany Key necklace.

There's a contest every month!

Visit www.1001DarkNights.com/key to subscribe.

As a bonus, all newsletter subscribers will receive a free
1001 Dark Nights story:

The First Night
by Shayla Black, Lexi Blake & M.J. Rose

Turn the page for a full list of the
1001 Dark Nights fabulous novellas...

1001 Dark Nights

Visit www.1001DarkNights.com for more information

FOREVER WICKED
A Wicked Lovers Novella
by Shayla Black

CRIMSON TWILIGHT
A Krewe of Hunters Novella
by Heather Graham

CAPTURED IN SURRENDER
A MacKenzie Family Novella
by Liliana Hart

SILENT BITE: A SCANGUARDS WEDDING
A Scanguards Vampire Novella
by Tina Folsom

DUNGEON GAMES
A Masters and Mercenaries Novella
by Lexi Blake

AZAGOTH
A Demonica Novella
by Larissa Ione

NEED YOU NOW
by Lisa Renee Jones

SHOW ME, BABY
A Masters of the Shadowlands Novella
by Cherise Sinclair

ROPED IN
A Blacktop Cowboys ® Novella
by Lorelei James

TEMPTED BY MIDNIGHT
A Midnight Breed Novella
by Lara Adrian

THE FLAME
by Christopher Rice

CARESS OF DARKNESS
A Phoenix Brotherhood Novella
by Julie Kenner

Also from Evil Eye Concepts:
TAME ME
A Stark International Novella
by J. Kenner

About Tina Folsom

Tina Folsom is a New York Times and USA Today Bestselling Author. She's always been self-published and has found tremendous success with her paranormal series, Scanguards Vampires, Venice Vampyr, and Out of Olympus, selling more than 1.5 million copies of her 50 titles (which includes titles in German, French, and Spanish) in almost 4 years.

Tina writes about hot alpha heroes, bad boys, and kick-ass heroines. Fast-paced plots and steamy scenes are her specialty. She loves vampires and the concept of immortality.

Tina is a one-women-enterprise. She writes constantly, translates her own books into German, her native language, and manages all aspects of her publishing empire. Her books are available in ebook format, as paperbacks, as audio books, and in foreign languages. She doesn't plan on stopping there and is constantly working on new and innovative ways to bring her books to more readers worldwide.

For more about Tina Folsom:

http://www.tinawritesromance.com

http://www.twitter.com/Tina_Folsom

http://www.facebook.com/TinaFolsomFans

You can also email her at tina@tinawritesromance.com

Tina is a member of the Indie Voice, a group of 10 New York Times bestselling indie authors who love recommending indie books. If you want to receive **information on great books and bargains**, and be entered in the **Indie Voice's monthly raffle (gift cards, e-readers, and other great prizes)**, please sign up for our newsletter on our website:

THE INDIE VOICE

Oliver's Hunger
Scanguards Vampires #7
Copyright © 2013 by Tina Folsom

There was a fire escape. She'd noticed it one night when one of the vampires had opened the blackened window at the end of the corridor where it made a bend to the right. It was her only chance.

She ran for it, stumbling several times until she reached it. Frantically, she tried to push the lower portion of the old sash window up, but it didn't move. Panic surged through her. Had they nailed it shut? She jerked on it again, this time more violently. Her breath deserted her and she dropped her head.

Why? Why? she cursed inwardly and slammed her small fist against the frame.

Then her eyes fell on the metal mechanism on top of the frame. The window was latched. It was one of those old latches from decades ago that simply held the window shut with a small lever one pushed from one side to the other; no key was needed.

Throwing a look over her shoulder, she quickly unlatched the window, then pushed it up. Cool night air drifted into the sticky corridor, making her shiver instantly. Her gaze fell onto the metal platform that was built outside the small window. The fire escape hung from it.

With haste, she squeezed through the open window and set her feet onto the platform, testing whether it would hold her. It bent under her weight, making her glance at the bolts that secured it to the building. It was too dark to see much, but she would bet that the metal was rusty.

Grabbing the handrail, she took her first hesitant step, then another one. Then she set a foot on the metal ladder, descending one story, then another. At the second floor, she stopped. The ladder came to an end.

Panicked she surveyed the platform, then discovered a stack of metal that appeared as if it was a ladder that had been gathered up. She kicked her foot against it, but it didn't move. Shouldn't it go all the way down to the ground?

Gingerly, she stepped on it, putting more weight onto what appeared to be the bottom step. Her hand grabbed the rail next to her, and underneath her fingers she felt a hook. She pulled on it.

All hell broke loose. The ladder released instantly, coming down with a loud thump, taking her with it as her feet continued resting on the last step. The freefall made adrenaline race through her veins, but seconds later she came to a dead stop, jerking her body forward. A metal rod snapped, slicing into her upper arm. Pain radiated through her, and she slammed her hand over the wound, trying to soothe the pain away.

But there was no time to lose now. The vampires would have heard the noise and would investigate.

Blindly, she ran out of the alley and into the next street. She didn't know where she was. When she and the other girls had been brought to this place it had been night, and they had been herded from a dark windowless truck into the building without getting a chance at seeing their surroundings. She didn't even know what city she was in.

Passing by a sign for an import/export company, she dashed into the next street, running as fast as she could. The streets were deserted, as if the area wasn't frequented by humans. Somewhere in the distance she heard cars, but still she saw nobody.

As she ran, she tried to take in her surroundings and make mental notes of street signs and buildings she passed.

Her lungs burned from exhaustion, her arm hurt from its encounter with the metal rod, and she could still feel blood trickling down her neck. If she couldn't close those wounds soon, she'd bleed out. She had to find help. At the same time she had to get away as far as possible from her captors, because they were like bloodhounds. They would smell her blood and be able to track her down.

Turning into the next street, she didn't slow her furious sprint. She was running on empty, and she knew it. But she wouldn't give up. She'd come this far, and freedom was just around the next corner. She couldn't let it slip through her fingers. Not when she was so close.

Before her eyes, everything became blurred, and she realized instantly that the blood loss was robbing her of her remaining strength. She stumbled, then caught herself. Her hands got hold of something soft. Thick fabric. Her fingers clawed at it, then hands pulled her up.

"What the fuck?" a male voice cursed.

"Help me," she begged. "They're after me. They're hunting me."

"Leave me alone," the stranger ordered and held her away at arm's length.

She lifted her head and looked at him for the first time. He was young, barely older than herself. Attractive too, if she could even make that kind of judgment in her foggy state of mind. His hair was dark and somewhat ruffled, his eyes piercing, his lips full and red.

Despite his words, he hadn't let go of her arms, supporting her weight which would have made her knees buckle otherwise.

Looking straight into his stunning blue eyes, she pleaded again, "Help me, please, I'll give you anything you want. Just get me out of here. To the next police station. Please!"

She needed help. Not just for herself, but also for the other girls. They had promised each other that whoever managed to escape would send help for the others.

His eyes narrowed a fraction as his forehead creased. His nostrils flared. "What's going on?"

"They're hunting me. You have to help me."

Suddenly his hands clamped tighter around her upper arms, and the pain in her wound intensified.

"Who's hunting you?" he hissed.

She couldn't tell him the truth, because the truth was too fantastic.

He wouldn't believe her, he'd think she was some crazy junkie if she told him about the vampires. Still, she needed his assistance. "Please help me! I'll do anything."

He looked at her intensely, his eyes boring into her, almost as if he was trying to determine whether she was drunk or crazy, or both.

"Please. Do you have a car?"

She noticed his eyes briefly wander to a dark minivan parked at the side of the road. "Why?"

"Because I've got to get away from here. Or they'll find me." She darted nervous looks over her shoulder. So far, the vampires hadn't caught up with her, but they couldn't be far behind. But she also noticed that this man was still the only one in the vicinity. If he didn't help her, she wouldn't make it. She couldn't run any longer.

"Listen, I'm not interested in whatever trouble you're in. I've got my own." He released her arms, and she would have fallen, had she not quickly gripped the lapels of his coat.

He glared at her. "I said—"

Desperation made her say words she thought she'd never utter. "I'll sleep with you if you help me."

He stopped dead in his movements, his eyes suddenly traveling over her, his nostrils flaring once more. Afraid that he would find something he didn't like, she slung her arms around his neck and pulled his head to her. Her lips found his an instant later.

Also from Tina Folsom

Visit http://www.tinawritesromance.com for more information

Tina's books are available in English, German, French, Spanish, as well as in audio.

Samson's Lovely Mortal (Scanguards Vampires #1)

Amaury's Hellion (Scanguards Vampires #2)

Gabriel's Mate (Scanguards Vampires #3)

Yvette's Haven (Scanguards Vampires #4)

Zane's Redemption (Scanguards Vampires #5)

Quinn's Undying Rose (Scanguards Vampires #6)

Oliver's Hunger (Scanguards Vampires #7)

Thomas's Choice (Scanguards Vampires #8)

A Touch of Greek (Out of Olympus #1)

A Scent of Greek (Out of Olympus #2)

A Taste of Greek (Out of Olympus #3)

Lover Uncloaked (Stealth Guardians #1)

Venice Vampyr #1

Venice Vampyr #2 Final Affair

Venice Vampyr #3 Sinful Treasure

Venice Vampyr #4 Sensual Danger

Lawful Escort

Lawful Lover

Lawful Wife: *coming in spring 2014*

The Wrong Suitor

Steal Me

Captured to Breed

Audio Books

Visit http://www.tinawritesromance.com for more information.

On behalf of 1001 Dark Nights,
Liz Berry and M.J. Rose would like to thank ~

Doug Scofield
Steve Berry
Richard Blake
Dan Slater
Asha Hossain
Chris Graham
Kim Guidroz
BookTrib After Dark
Jillian Stein
and Simon Lipskar

CPSIA information can be obtained at www.ICGtesting.com
Printed in the USA
LVOW11s1521030915

452709LV00005B/670/P